UNLEASH THE FURY

A STORM OF VENGEANCE ON EASTERN SANDS

JOSEPH PAUL D'AQUISTO

OTHER BOOKS BY
JOSEPH PAUL D'AQUISTO:

- *Left For Death*

This book is dedicated to the late Joseph Paul D'Aquisto Sr.
I will never forget you.
May you forever rest in peace.
(1941-2002)

CHAPTER 1

Life, sometimes, is amusing. No matter how good or bad things get, there are still sides, and you end up choosing one. You go in one direction, trying to come to terms with the decision, thinking in your mind that maybe you should've done things differently. Either way, you could end up dead before you know it. I had spent the majority of my later years alone. Retirement made my life much calmer, but at times also dull. Transitioning to private investigations helped maintain a sense of purpose in my life. I liked to relax as much as anyone else, but all play and no work was not something I could be content with.

• • •

I awoke promptly at six o'clock in the morning, stretched my arms above my head, and let out a long yawn. Minutes later, I was sipping a large cup of joe and staring out the window. I took a slow swallow—inhaling the aroma through my nostrils. I finished the coffee a few minutes later, let out a long relaxing breath, set the cup down, and headed to the shower.

I stared at my body in the mirror. I had lost the stomach flab that had been plaguing me for most of my fifties and sixties by upping the exercise and watching what I ate. My belly was flat, although the soft pudge would start to come back once in a while if I ate or drank too much. But I had been attentive. A few years ago, I had weighed about two hundred pounds, which, at that time, had been my highest weight ever. Now, I weighed even more—two hundred and ten—but looked thinner due to increased exercising and diet changes. Most days, I did a minimum of fifty push-ups and sit-ups. I added more daily walking exercises, joined a local gym, and started taking swim classes. I didn't lift weights too much, but the slight adjustments had still made a big difference.

I turned on the hot water and soaked my body, the hot steam slowly waking me up. I stood there for a good sixty seconds—just letting the water run down me. I dried myself off and picked up the small can of Barbasol to lather my face and neck, then slowly brought the razor down until I had removed all of the several days of stubble. I got dressed and walked through the living room to the small kitchen, took a water bottle and a few pieces of fruit from the fridge, sat down in a chair, and ate in silence for several minutes, just staring off into space.

An hour later, it was just past seven thirty, and I was walking on the warm white shore of Galle Beach, wearing thin khaki pants, a light short-sleeved collared shirt, and brown boots. It was the beginning of January 2009. I had retired from the Seattle Police Department a little over three years ago, where I had been a detective for many years. Within a matter of months, I started doing freelance investigations. Most of the cases weren't anything exciting—typical divorce cases, tax fraud investigations. Some high-profile cases came up occasionally, such as the kidnapping of a politician's daughter. I had quickly gotten to the bottom of that one, exposing a group of young hooligans trying to extort some quick cash from a wealthy public figure. At sixty-nine, I was more than glad to be done with the police department.

Never having been outside the western hemisphere my entire life, I decided on a trip to Sri Lanka and had been on vacation for the last month. Since my arrival, I'd been staying in a small apartment in the Galle Beach area. Except for flying in through Colombo, I had not seen any part of the rest of the country. Later today, I planned to explore, possibly east around Dondra. I'd check out of my apartment and load my one suitcase and small backpack into my rental car. It was great to travel light and not worry about lugging around a bunch of crap like most tourists.

I was happy to finally be able to see some of the exotic places I'd always wondered about. The weather was warm, about eighty-five degrees, which was a hell of a lot warmer than Seattle. As far as I was concerned, I had no desire to go back to Seattle or anywhere in the rainy Pacific Northwest any time soon. I felt a little sweat running down my legs despite my thin pants so I rolled my pant cuffs up a little. No matter the temperature, I never wore shorts. Even when I went jogging, I would wear light warm-up pants. The only time I wore shorts was when I went swimming, making sure to quickly change back into some sort of pants. I felt uncomfortable showing my legs for some reason. It felt weird to me. It had taken me a while to get over my fear of exposing my legs, even for short durations. I had regularly gone swimming here at the beach, but I always had to run back and put on some long pants once I stepped out of that water. Maybe it's silly, but that's me.

I glanced around, embracing the beautiful view of the bright blue ocean water and lovely palm trees. Walking around for quite some time, I realized it was almost eleven o'clock. I needed some food, and maybe an alcoholic beverage. It had been several days since my last libation. Being on vacation, I had consumed more than I probably should have. I felt as fit as a fiddle. Cheating a little on food and beverage wouldn't hurt me too badly. I slapped my mostly hard abs with my hand as I walked toward the nearby beach restaurant. I studied the menu at the door, noticing the Indian and Asian cuisine assortment. A few minutes later, a young man who looked like he may have been Sinhalese seated me. He asked if I would like to sit inside or outside. I chose the outside patio. The inside looked too crowded, and besides, I enjoyed the fresh ocean air.

I was escorted to a table and told someone would be with me shortly. A young brunette was sitting by herself two tables over. I gazed across the patio. I spotted a man appearing to be in his eighties who was reading a newspaper while holding a drink, also alone. The slight breeze in the air felt good. A different young man came by to take my order, a scotch on the rocks, which once again broke my dietary habits. The man returned and set the scotch down. I picked up the glass, took a sip, and swished it around my mouth before swallowing. I took a deep breath and let it out slowly.

A few minutes later, a different waiter came over and took my food order. I ordered a local noodle dish with an assortment of vegetables with spices. It had a bit of an odd taste, hard for my taste buds to get used to. My stomach missed familiar American food. Another hour later, I finished, paid my bill, and walked back to my apartment to check out. I was ready to hit the road and further explore this foreign land.

• • •

I stared at myself in the rearview; my madras hat was on, and my face was clean-shaven. I felt pretty damn good as I headed east to Dondra by car.

Mehliana, the area I had pulled into, was a one-horse town, not very impressive. Thirty to forty minutes west of where I was heading, it was right along the water. Dirt streets and run-down buildings, there was not much to look at. One thing was sure. It wasn't on any official maps. I had spent my fair share of time in Podunk towns, but deep down, no matter what I tried to tell myself, I was a city man at heart. I liked paved roads to stand on and bright lights to gaze at during the night. This little blink of an eye was a place to fill up, get a quick bite to eat, and maybe spend the night if you had no other choice. I parked my car just off the road in front of a shabby-looking fuel station with a restaurant attached to it. A few other assorted businesses and establishments were short walking distance; many looked closed. I took my madras hat off, threw it in the back seat, and exited the vehicle. I made my way to the restaurant entrance.

Then I happened to stare in her direction, which marked the exact time the shitshow started. The woman was short, frail, dark brown complexion and dark hair, and looked in her midtwenties. Two men escorted her, one at each side grabbing an arm. The three of them were exiting the restaurant as I approached. She struggled to break free from their grip, yelling at both men. They gave me a hard stare. I stared back.

"Hey. It doesn't seem like the lady wants to go with either of you guys," I said.

One of the men, heavyset and big-boned, a few inches taller than me, with dark greasy hair, snapped, "You should learn to mind your own fucking business, mister."

By now, the woman was shrieking. The other man was behind her, holding her tight to his chest. He dragged her several more feet toward one of the parked cars. Several people were standing inside the doorway of the restaurant watching. The man who had snapped at me opened the trunk and pulled out a large plastic water bottle.

"You think you can leave me, woman! You are my property! You belong to me! You do not leave me!"

He took the cap off the bottle and threw water in her face as the other man still held her arms from behind. She screamed in agony.

"No! No! Help!" She fell to the dirt ground, holding her arms to her face.

"Hey, you son of a bitch!" I screamed, instantly charging at the man. But he threw me to the ground and jumped on top of me. He landed a hard punch right to my face. I struggled to throw his heavy frame off me. The other man kicked me from behind as I got up, knocking me back down. They both kicked me repeatedly into the dirt several times.

"I told you to mind your own fucking business!" the big man said. "This doesn't concern you. You're lucky I don't kill you right here and now, you old geezer."

After a moment, the men finally stopped and shifted their focus back to the woman. "Now you can think about your actions, you fucking bitch," the big man said as he and the other man walked away down the street. I saw them go into another building about three or four buildings down. The woman, still on the ground, was howling in pain. The fuel attendant, along with several of the patrons in the restaurant, poured water over her face. One of the staff members came out carrying another large container of water and started running it slowly over the head of the poor woman, who was still screaming.

My body was covered in dirt when I got up. Despite some scrapes and cuts, I hadn't suffered any significant injuries. I stumbled in horror toward the woman and the crowd helping her. Her face looked nothing at all like it had moments earlier. It was now entirely charred, like she had just fallen into a volcano. Only burned skin with uneven coloring remained, with half of her hair gone. One of her earlobes had disintegrated. A piece of the bone from her skull was now visible on the back of her head. I strained to get a good look at her face and saw her eyes were out of position.

"I can't see! I can't see! Why! Why did you do this to me!" she cried hysterically.

My heart was beating uncontrollably fast. It was that moment that I realized the liquid splashed in her face wasn't water, but acid. I bent down, placing both hands on my knees, trying to think. I stood up again. I wanted to intervene and talk with the woman, but she was in no position to do so. I watched the people continue to soak her with water and gently comfort her. All I could do was stare.

"I should have done something," I said to myself softly.

"Dad, you can't blame yourself for that. It happened so suddenly. There's no way you would have known this would happen," Mallory said.

"I'm law enforcement. I should've reacted sooner."

"You retired three years ago. You're on vacation."

"I should've protected her. Just like I should have protected you. In both cases, I failed. I'm a miserable excuse for a human being. I love you, Mallory."

"I love y—"

"Excuse me, mister, are you okay? Who are you talking to?"

I looked over, snapping back into reality. One of the restaurant workers was standing next to me. He was a younger, thin man about my height, in his early twenties with dark skin and hair.

"No one. Yes, I'm fine. Where's the nearest police station?" I asked him.

"The local station is just down the street." He pointed in the same direction the two men had walked. "But don't expect much out of them. As you can see, this is a lawless territory."

I walked away from the man without responding.

CHAPTER 2

It took me less than a minute to find the police station. I walked up the wooden steps onto the deck—every building here had a deck. I reached the front entrance, stopped, and stared behind me, the crowd at the restaurant down the street visible from this vantage point. I entered the double doors to find a pair of men sitting at their respective desks on either side, each staring at me in amusement. The men looked as if they were waiting for me. Nothing was exciting about the interior. It's common for police stations to have lots of paper forms, office supplies, award plaques, and such. This was not the case here. I just saw a place where people hung out. Near the far corner of the room, I spotted several liquor bottles on an empty desk.

I took a few steps to the middle of the room, pointing outside. Before I could utter a word, the man on the left side of the room stood up. He was a relatively tall man, maybe six-two, midthirties, lanky, sporting a small black mustache, and balding on top.

"Oh, I saw it. Was that why you came in here? You're the one who got in a tussle with Adeepa. He threw you to the ground like a rag doll. And the other guy—Radawa. He even joined the party. I could see it all happening. All I had to do was look out the window. And you know what I'm going to do? Not one goddamn thing. But I know what you should do if you know what's good for you. You should take your ass back outside, walk back to your vehicle, and just drive out of town. What do you think, Kanish?" He looked over to the man still seated, who nodded without speaking.

"You have to excuse Inspector General Kanish here. He doesn't speak much. Oh, I just realized I forgot to introduce myself. I'm Senior Deputy Inspector Raj Khan, in case you wanted to take down notes," he said, a shit-eating grin on his face. "Now, if you decide not to take my advice and end up lingering around here longer, then listen here, and listen damn good. Do not—I repeat—do not come here expecting help. This town is every man for himself. Those guys you got into a scrap with, they're with the Sri Lankan mob. They run this town. Uvindu Singh is the man who heads it. Adeepa is probably Singh's second-best guy after Lasal, who, luckily, you haven't met yet. The other gang is a group of Aussies on the other side of town. They're led by William James. They're a different type of bunch but no less dangerous than any of Singh's boys."

I looked into this so-called lawman's eyes. A fake, a pushover. He wasn't worth wasting my time with.

"Thanks for the warm welcome. I guess I'll stay a little while." I could tell that comment irked each of them. I turned my back and walked to the door.

"Oh, one more thing!" Khan barked.

I turned to him.

"You should get yourself a gun. You might live longer that way."

Then I walked out. Little did he know, little did he know.

CHAPTER 3

The crowd had dissipated. I overheard someone say the woman had been driven to the nearest hospital. I walked back to my car, drove a block away, and parked in an isolated spot. I needed some time to think. I came here to get away from all the darkness in my life. I had flown to the other side of the world to escape. I thought I could move on, but trouble had a way of following me. It had been only three years earlier that I had found out my former supervisor police chief had been in cahoots with a child sex trafficking ring. Fucking Larry, Marlboro Man, and all the goddamned rest of the rat bastards. I still thought about Marlboro Man all these years after he disappeared. He had gotten away, and it was all my fault.

Every day passed, and I got older and older. Despite feeling physically better the last few years, I wasn't invincible. I was still alone. The longer I went on, the less connected I felt to anyone and anything. *What purpose do I have? Does anything even matter anymore?* I sighed, leaned my head back against the seat, and took a deep breath. *If I die today, will anyone care?* I continued staring off into space for a few more moments. I thought further about what I was about to do. *Am I making the right decision?* There was still time to change my mind and do what the deputy inspector suggested. It would be easy enough to bolt out of this dump of a town. No. I had to stay. If I left like a coward, I would be allowing criminals to escape again. After what I had just seen, I simply couldn't run away.

I reached under my seat and pulled out a small hard gun case. Inside were two all-black Glock G17 handguns. When arriving in Sri Lanka, the first thing I did was visit a gun shop. It was best not to bring any weapons on the plane, and firearms were easy to purchase once I arrived in the country. I had always carried a handgun throughout my time with the police and during my freelancing these recent years. I felt more comfortable having one on me, even more so after what I had just witnessed those two men do to that defenseless woman. Each gun had a full magazine, seventeen plus one in the chamber. In addition, I had four extra, fully loaded magazines in the box. I reached under the seat again and pulled out a box of bullets. Two guns with a full mag each would be enough. I pulled out a double shoulder holster from the glove compartment, put it on, and secured my guns at each side. I grabbed a thin blazer from the back seat and exited the car, leaving my madras hat so I wouldn't lose it. I put the blazer on to conceal my firearms and then walked back toward the central area of town. I didn't see exactly which building Adeepa and Radawa had entered, but I was sure the three of us would find each other one way or another.

• • •

Once I returned in front of the restaurant, I looked around in all directions. I stared at the fuel station, back at the restaurant, the police station, and then again down the street, trying to retrace Adeepa and Radawa's steps. They couldn't have been more than four buildings away. I walked slowly and steadily, peering from left to right. Finally, I spotted a few guys outside one of the buildings to my left. I headed in their direction. I got about twenty steps further before they finally spotted me.

"I'm looking for Adeepa."

"Who the hell are you?" one of the men asked.

"Just someone who wants to talk."

"Adeepa! Some jerk-off foreigner who thinks he's a tough guy is here to see you!" the man called out.

A few seconds later, Adeepa's sturdy build appeared at the top of the front steps, and he glared down at me.

"What the fuck do you want?!" he yelled.

"That was a bad thing you did back there. I think you need to pay for what you did to that poor woman."

Adeepa and the rest of the men roared with laughter. He came down the steps and stopped about fifteen feet from me.

"Ha ha! Yeah? Who's going to make me do that? You?"

"I guess I'll have to teach you a lesson."

"Then I guess you'll have to kill me."

"It'll hurt if I do."

He stared for a moment into my eyes before suddenly reaching his right hand into the left side of his coat. He had barely gotten his gun out when I quickly brought both guns out from their holsters.

Three shots from each gun fired into his chest. As each bullet struck his body, his heavy frame jiggled. Upon landing, he thudded hard on the dirt. He was dead as a doornail. I aimed my guns at the other men. I counted three guys plus Radawa, who I hadn't spotted outside until that very second.

"You want some too?" I screamed at them. "I'll shoot all of you right here and now!"

I was game for more shooting, but they were all down on the ground with their hands raised.

"You tell Mr. Singh that none of this would've happened if he had better guys working for him."

I stepped backward with my guns still aimed at the men until I was a reasonable enough distance away at the end of the block. I ran away as fast as I could, got back to my car, hopped in, and drove off.

CHAPTER 4

I drove several miles out of town to nowhere in particular. I parked in a deserted area underneath several palm trees to gather my thoughts. The shade from the trees helped a bit with the heat. I made sure to fully reload each of my firearms. Leaving now would be impossible. The point of no return had been reached, and the fight was far from over. I had avenged that poor woman, but it wouldn't take away her pain and suffering. Her life was ruined. As for me, it was too late, and I knew it. I probably wasn't going to make it out of this fiasco, but I'd make damn well sure I went down swinging. I felt invigorated, as if I had a duty to take on this corrupt force. These were the things that kept me going. I managed to calm myself a bit, making my way back to the town center. I did not want to show anyone I was scared, so I parked back in front of the fuel station and restaurant. I glanced around to see Deputy Inspector Khan standing outside the police station smoking a cigarette. He was staring right at me. *Good. I'm glad.* If he wanted to come after me, then so be it. The quicker to end it all, the better. The fuel attendant stared at me as I walked past him into the restaurant. There was only one worker on duty, the young guy who had talked to me earlier. There were no other patrons inside.

"Oh my God. It's you! Would you like a meal on the house? A drink? Anything you want," he said.

I gave him a puzzled look.

"Maybe a scotch on the rocks and a medium-rare steak if you have it, but I'll pay you," I replied.

"Oh no, it's on me. I can't believe you dropped Adeepa like that. Besides, you may not be around much longer after what you did. People are going to be looking for you. The whole town is talking about it. Everyone's gossiping," the young man said. He seemed way more excited than he should've been.

I gave him another stare. "Who's 'everyone'?" I asked. "How many people does this town even have anyway? A hundred?"

"Singh is out of town, I heard, headed back tonight. The word even got out to William James and his men."

"Is that right?"

"Damn right. I wouldn't be surprised if James tried to hire you as a gunman," he said, continuing to act like a thrilled little schoolboy.

I contemplated for a moment—tried figuring out a plan with my newfound fame. At least people now knew I was no pushover.

"Do you have a phone in this place? I bought a mobile phone here a while back, but it's useless in this country. No signal anywhere."

"Who are you trying to call?"

This guy sure was nosy. "My mommy." I smirked, trying to keep my calm façade.

He snorted at my reply. "We have landline phones, but they don't work either. This town isn't good for much. We don't have any people to service anything. Most of the good people have come and gone. It's an abandoned town except for the gangs and a small handful of others. Hell, I'm surprised the fuel attendant hasn't run off yet. Those cowardly inspectors at the police station stay in the middle taking kickbacks from both sides to keep their mouths shut. Both gangs arrived within a couple of months of each other several years back, but they don't get along very well. James and his group are mostly smuggling drugs in and out of Australia. Singh's operations are a little more complex. They're equally dangerous, though."

At the bar, I positioned myself so that my back was not facing the entrance.

"These guys all live around here?" I asked curiously

"Most of Singh's group stays just down the street in and around where you shot Adeepa. James's crew is holed up at the big Kundali hotel on the far side of town. Generally, if you stay out of their way, both gangs will leave you be, but you've pretty much fucked yourself with Singh." He gritted his teeth and gave me a cringed look.

"How long will that steak take? I'm hungry. Could eat a horse."

"Oh, I know a supplier that can get horse mea—"

I put my hand up, shaking my finger. "No, no. A figure of speech. Just get me a steak, will you?"

"I'll get working on it right now. Here's your scotch. Oh, I'm Calvin, by the way," he said as he set my drink down.

"John." I nodded my head at him.

I took a large pull of the scotch. Calvin disappeared into the kitchen. About fifteen to twenty minutes later, he set down the steak in front of me. I cut into it and took my first bite when the doors flew open. Three white men stepped inside. The youngest-looking among them appeared to be in his late twenties. He was kind of short, maybe five-eight, medium build, red hair, and clean-shaven. The other two were taller, over six feet, both with brown hair, each around thirty-five, forty years old. One had a beard and the other clean-shaven.

"Are you the one? It's got to be you!" the young one said.

"The one what?" I retorted, taking another bite of my meal.

"Oh, it's him! It's definitely him! I can tell he's a tough one!"

Suddenly, the man with the beard shoved the young man out of the way. "Shut up, Randy. I'm Jim. The talky one here is Randy, and this here is Bob," he said, gesturing to the third man. "Now, what's your name?"

"John."

"John? I don't suppose you have a last name, John?" he snickered.

"Just John."

"Where you from, John?"

"Out west."

He gave an amused laugh and said, "Ha. Out west. You're American. Okay, then. William James would like to invite you over for a business meeting."

This was not what I expected, but Calvin had sure called it. I had to keep my wits about me, but this might be in my favor. I guess I'd play along if it kept me alive longer. Despite several opportunities to get the hell out of Dodge, I wasn't running away. I wanted to learn more about what was going on here, but I made sure not to seem overly interested.

"Guess I can't say no, can I?" I sneered.

"Well, you most certainly could, but I wouldn't recommend it. We've already heard Singh's crew is plotting to take you out sometime in the next day or so. Not coming with us would be stupid."

"But I just started on my steak," I said, displaying an annoyed look.

"Forget the steak. There's plenty of good food at the Kundali. C'mon."

I downed my scotch, took one last bite of my steak, and stood up.

"See you around, Calvin." I nodded at him again.

He gave me a wave, a concerned look on his face as if he wanted to say something.

The four of us exited the restaurant, got into a dark green Jeep Wrangler with tinted windows, and sped off. We drove right past the police station, where both inspectors stood near the doorway, looking in our direction. As we passed by the building where I'd killed Adeepa just hours earlier, I saw that the body had been moved. At least eight or nine Sri Lankan men stood around, and they gave us all a hard stare. No doubt, they were pissed.

I was in the back of the Jeep, seated next to Randy.

He turned to me "You scared?"

"Do I look scared?"

"Not even a little?"

I shrugged. I was maybe a little scared.

CHAPTER 5

"What in the hell were you thinking when you went up to Adeepa and all his guys like that?" William James said, laughing along with the rest of the men seated at the long table.

James was blond with blue eyes, tall at nearly six-four, and possessed a fit but lean build. I guessed his weight to be around two hundred and thirty pounds. He had a pretty boy look to him, the kind that most ladies probably went crazy over.

There were twelve of us in total at the table. James was seated at the head, and I was to his immediate right. There were four men to my right side and five more across the other side of the table. I didn't bother learning everyone's name, as it was way too easy to forget them. Their names didn't matter to me, just their faces.

A woman who I guessed to be either James's wife, girlfriend, or mistress sat at the other end of the table. Her demeanor was much quieter than the men's. She was about five-ten, slender, a brunette with pale skin and green eyes, who wore a sleeveless dark blue cami dress. She had a thin gold chain around her neck and diamond earrings.

"I saw them splash acid in that poor woman's face, so I decided to have a little talk with them," I replied coolly.

"You sure did," a man across from me said as the entire table burst into laughter again.

"Singh and his damn acid attacks. It's a common tactic on this side of the world, unfortunately, particularly from jealous men directed at women," James said. "Just forget about that. You're with us now, on the right side, the winning side." He flashed his pearly whites.

A real winner, all right, I chuckled to myself.

Being a stranger in a strange and hostile land hadn't gotten me a warm welcome here, and the fact that I had quickly offed a top mafia thug only made it worse. However, the longer I started thinking about it, the more I felt I might use this situation to learn about this town's happenings. The question was, what exactly? So far, there were two corrupt lawmen willing to look the other way and two criminal groups that hated each other. My only worry was that more innocent people would get harmed. I decided to continue playing my hand—whatever that meant.

As the night wore on, the men got louder and drunker. I made sure to be conservative with my alcoholic intake. I listened to them talk and learned more about their drug smuggling operation. Everything got moved out of Sydney to here. James ran a family operation, and most of his workers were distant relatives or close friends. He was very selective about who he let into his business ventures, or so he said.

"So, we've been at odds with Singh's guys for years, but for the past several months, we've had a sort of—" James started to explain.

"Cease-fire!" Randy, always the loudmouth, blurted.

Jim smacked him on the side of his head. "Shut up, Randy." He looked back at James and said, "This truce isn't going to last, especially after Lasal gets back with Singh. He's out of town."

"That's why we called him out here," James said, pointing in my direction.

"I've heard this Lasal is kind of a big deal," I said.

"Lasal is Singh's top guy," James said. "He's a real character. That's for sure. But don't worry about him. Hey, where'd you say you were from again?" James was testing me to see if I'd lower my guard with the alcohol. I didn't fall for it.

"I didn't."

James chuckled. "Yeah, all right. You're obviously American, but from where exactly who the hell knows. You running from something?"

I shrugged. "Maybe. Maybe not."

• • •

A few hours later, everyone had finished their meals and drinks, and several men got up to leave. James stayed behind along with two other guys and the girl. She had looked bored and uninterested during all the drunken man-talk.

"All right, enough with the small talk," James said. "I invited you here 'cause I wanted to see if you wanted to jump in on my drug smuggling operation." He paused. And here it was, the job offer.

"I've got a big shipment coming in three days. Saturday evening, to be exact. The delivery will happen just a little west of here, near Dondra. I could use a guy like you. We need gunmen in case Singh's goons try to pull anything. I don't trust him, and you've been pretty good in your short time here with taking out Adeepa. I'm sure that we could drop his guys left and right with you on our crew. Trust me, I got the good shit. Singh has some drugs, too, but mine are top-notch. Grade A heroin."

I stayed silent for a moment, wondering what he'd think if he knew I was a retired police detective. On the other hand, the local police here were scumbags anyway, so he probably wouldn't flinch.

"Look, John, let me level with you. These are high-quality goods." He turned his head to the hallway and said, "Bob! Where's the kid? Go fetch him." He snapped his fingers, and Bob peeked his head into the room, nodded, and left.

Bob returned with a frail-looking boy a few minutes later, probably no more than fifteen. He looked sluggish and malnourished.

"Ramal, nice to see you!" James greeted the kid. "Have a seat."

"No, I think his name's Rahish," Bob countered as he helped sit the boy into a chair right next to James, the one across from me.

"My name is Lem—" the boy started.

"Who gives a shit? I got some stuff for you to sample." James pulled a small packet of white powder from his pocket, slapping it down directly in front of him. "Somebody hand me a clean spoon and a syringe."

One of the men handed James what he'd requested. He used the spoon to scoop a small amount of the powder from the packet. Reaching into his pocket again, he pulled out a lighter and ignited the bottom of the spoon. He kept it lit to let the product cook. A moment later, he filled the syringe with the now liquefied substance and handed it to the boy. The poor kid was too weak to even hold it properly. His eyes were bloodshot, and he looked like he hadn't eaten or slept in days. His shaking arms were skinny as rails and had needle marks all over them. Several times, he tried unsuccessfully to find a vein on his arm. It was hard for me not to wince.

"Bob, do it for him, dammit," James, getting impatient, commanded.

Bob grabbed the kid's little arm and held it firmly in place. He tapped on it until he found a vein and then shot him up. The kid's eyes rolled to the back of his head.

"How's the product, son?" James asked him.

"Very good. The gateway to heaven has opened for me," the kid whispered with a sudden change to euphoric expression.

"What did I tell you? Good shit. I only sell the best."

Everything I had just witnessed sickened me. This poor kid was near the brink of death.

James stared at me. "Don't worry, he can handle it. He always does. So, what else is going on in the world?"

They left that kid in the chair to experience his high, ignoring him for the remainder of the evening. I glanced at him several times. He wouldn't last long. Death would come for him soon. I could feel it. He would be left for death, and there was nothing I could do for him right now. I wanted to do something, but I looked deep into my dark thoughts and imagined myself as nothing more than an empty soul. *Hold your emotions in check, John. You must control yourself to see this through. Breathe!* I had a part to play. I glanced once more at the kid. His eyes were now closed, and I had to finally turn away. I chose to look at the girl. Not wanting to look at the poor kid or the stupid goons, I figured she was the best thing—or should I say, person—to stare at. She had a severe expression on her face, obviously not amused at anything happening. James noticed me staring, mistakenly thinking I was showing interest in her.

"Hey, Lana, come over here." He waved her over.

"Yeah, I'm coming. Hold your horses," Lana said nonchalantly, walking from the other side of the table.

I was instantly reminded of my prior conversation with Calvin today about the horse. I chuckled slightly out loud.

James stared at me, confused, and asked, "What's amusing you?"

"Nothing important. I'm impressed with your operation," I lied. I was anything but impressed. I was revolted.

Lana slowly approached—a very unenthusiastic look on her face.

"What's wrong, baby? Am I inconveniencing you? This is Lana. She's a good girl. She's got a bitchy attitude sometimes, but if she gets too out of hand, I won't hesitate to smack that pretty mouth of hers shut." James gave her an annoyed glance. "Hey, it could be worse. Better than acid. Right, babe?" Lana stared down at the ground.

Initially, James had appeared to be a bit more refined than what I had seen from Adeepa and the Sri Lankans, but my mind had quickly changed over the past few hours. He was a piece of shit like the rest of them.

"Now, Lana, you're going to be very hospitable to our guest Mr. John here, and don't be a pain in the ass. Isn't that right, darling?"

"Yea, right," she answered, trying to appear indifferent, but I could sense her fear. Even with a guy like James, she was in way over her head.

"Now, take him and show him his room, please."

I hadn't planned on staying the night. The rest of my bullets were in my car back on the other side of town, but I had both guns fully loaded on me. I just hoped Singh or those crooked lawmen didn't screw with my vehicle. I got up, nodded at James, and exited the room with Lana. We ascended two flights of stairs to the third floor of the hotel.

"I guess James found another bum," she said as she hooked her arm around mine.

"I guess you know everything, huh?" I asked.

"Uh-huh. I'm a real psychic. Don't get me wrong, not everything James does is good, but being with him has its benefits."

"Maybe if you don't mind watching teens get shot up with drugs." I watched her wince at that last comment.

"Please, I'd rather not talk about that. You will like your room a lot." She led me to the door, kissed me on the cheek, and whispered, "Good night."

I closed the door and looked around. What the fuck was I doing? What was this woman's game anyway? I had no romantic interest in her whatsoever, but she was working me over for some reason. Suddenly the door opened up again, and her head popped in. I wheeled around, surprised.

"Oh. Try not to be too loud, okay? My room is directly below."

Thinking of the most ridiculous thing to say, I quickly recomposed myself back into character. I sneered, "I'll try not to make too much noise when I'm jumpin' up and down on my beddy bed." I smiled. She gave me a perplexed look. When she left again, I made sure to lock the door. "Beddy bed?" What the fuck was that? What a stupid thing to say. Something weird was happening to my mind, and I didn't know what.

That little dinner show had been quite the spectacle. At this point, I couldn't tell who I had to worry about more—James or Singh. Even though I had yet to lay eyes on Singh, I was concerned more with him and his crew. James still seemed small compared to Singh, but maybe I underestimated him. He had a lot of money in his pocket. I counted the men at the dinner table and the several others posted throughout the hotel. He had roughly twenty guys. Most of them seemed like silly goons, especially that punk kid, Randy. It was like straight out of some cheesy action thriller novel. Though I was still disturbed about what James had done with that poor kid. I sat up for a long while before eventually drifting off into a deep sleep.

CHAPTER 6

I was on the ground, along with everyone else in the building. "Don't anybody move, or I'll put a bullet in this bitch's head!" the man roared as he held a gun to the teller.

The bank was crowded with people. The robber had startled everyone when he barged in screaming. People were cowering in fear. He had a black ski mask over his face, but I could still see his wild hazel eyes. They were about fifty feet away from me. The young redhead in the robber's grip was terrified; her entire body shook uncontrollably. Sweat ran down her forehead. The rent-a-cop security man, who was much younger than me, had probably never experienced this sort of thing in his life. Sure enough, Barney Fife had a gun inside his coat, but I hoped he wouldn't make any stupid moves. An inexperienced security guard could get someone killed. The robber was leading the girl toward the vault.

"Where are the keys to the vault?" he asked the girl.

"Barbara, the supervisor, has them." She pointed to a slightly older brunette, who was on the ground near the counter.

"Go over to her and grab them! And don't try anything stupid!"

He continued to aim the pistol at the poor girl's head. Barbara handed over the keys.

"Lead the way to the vault and unlock it."

The bank robber pushed the girl from behind as they both walked down a hallway and disappeared out of sight. He was an amateur. No professional would leave the front unattended. It was at that moment that things started to go to hell. The rent-a-cop jumped up off the floor and pulled out his gun, moving quickly but clumsily. He stumbled over someone's leg as he tried hopping over people. His weapon hit the floor as it fell from his hand—immediately firing a shot into the wall.

"What the hell?" the robber said as he quickly reappeared. When the guard made a grab for his gun, the gunman fired with his pistol, hitting the poor guard on the right side of his abdomen. While collapsing onto his back, the guard groaned loudly. As the robber was shooting, the teller had returned from the vault, bolting for the door.

"You goddamn bitch!" he snarled as he aimed at the back of her head.

I was up in a flash. I reached for my firearm, but it wasn't there. The only thing I could do was run at the robber. Everything happened in slow motion as I felt my heart pound furiously. With all my strength and might, I ran. I felt as though I had been running for an entire minute. The robber looked even farther away than he had seconds before, and I saw him start to squeeze the trigger. This was impossible. How was he getting farther away? I ran faster toward him, tackling him at the exact moment bullets were released from the chamber. The robber went down like a sacked quarterback. I had my knee in the man's back, one hand grabbing his left wrist while holding his head down hard against the ground with my other.

Sirens sounded outside. Suddenly the building was flooded with cops. Officers surrounded the two of us and moved me away. They cuffed the robber's hands behind his back. I walked over to where the girl had fallen, but I couldn't see. A dozen cops were hovering near her. I squeezed through a couple of them only to find more blocking my way to her. I stepped between them, but there were many more. What the hell? How was this possible? The circle of cops had multiplied, and I seemed to be getting pushed farther away. I was enraged, and I blindly shoved cops out of my way. The moment seemed to go on forever. Finally, I could see the woman's legs, then her torso. A thick red pool surrounded her head. She was lying facedown, the back of her head missing. "Oh my God! The girl is dead. She's dead!" I screamed.

Shrieking laughter rattled my eardrums. I almost fell over from the agony it caused my head. I wheeled around to see the robber standing with two cops. He continued laughing, getting louder each second. His ski mask was still on, and his white teeth displayed a wide grin. He was looking right at me.

"Somebody take that goddamn mask off him!" I shouted, but no one seemed to hear.

I was breathing heavily. My head hurt, and I collapsed on the ground. I was on my knees, and the robber was still standing there, laughing. Laughing at the dead girl, laughing at me, laughing at the whole situation. Nobody paid attention to me on the ground. My head continued to throb. I remained still for a moment, desperately trying to regain my composure. The robber continued wildly laughing. I finally got up and went over to him. As I smashed my fist into his face, he cried out in pain. Blood was gushing from the robber's mouth as he moaned. There was a brief pause before he began to laugh again. I reached forward, grabbed the mask, and yanked it off his head.

CHAPTER 7

I suddenly awoke from a nightmare—dripping with sweat and breathing heavily. In recent years, they have become more frequent. I had no idea what this one meant. A bank robbery? Sometimes my dreams were memories, but this particular one wasn't. It was just a random one. However, one characteristic remained the same throughout them: my inability to resolve the issue. I didn't get much sleep, but the few hours I did get were pretty solid. While I usually did not get more than three to four hours of sleep a night, it was a plus when I had deep dreams, no matter how bizarre or alarming they were. I had both guns placed on the pillow beside me, and I kept waiting for a bunch of guys to burst in and have me whacked. I finally drifted off around two o'clock in the morning.

I woke up just after six. I stepped into the bathroom, rested my firearms on each side of the sink, and then showered. I let the hot water run over my body for a solid minute as per my usual routine. I needed to think through a way to end this little adventure I'd found myself in.

• • •

I was fully dressed at a quarter to seven and walked down the stairs to the kitchen. As I got to the ground floor, I heard several voices. James, four other men, and Lana were eating eggs and bacon with biscuits. There was no sign of the kid from last night.

"How'd you sleep, John?" James asked.

"Fine," I lied again.

"As you can see, we've got no short supply of Western food. Some of the local cuisines are all right, I guess, but it's nice to have a taste of home if you know what I mean." He was still trying to win me over. I took a seat at the table and helped myself to a serving. "Good, huh?"

I nodded. "Yeah, and it's peppered. I like pepper."

Suddenly, a man who I hadn't seen at dinner last night entered the kitchen and screamed, "Seriously? What the hell! We don't wait for each other anymore?"

"You're late, Sonny," James replied with an annoyed expression.

"I was dealing with stuff. I just got back from Australia. You know that!" Sonny snapped.

He was probably midthirties, olive skin, dark hair, brown eyes, medium build, and maybe six feet tall.

"While you were messing around in Oz, we got a bunch of shit going on here. This is John, our new employee. John, this is Sonny. This guy killed Adeepa. That's Singh's best guy after Lasal."

"Yeah, I heard. I was briefed on the way over from the airport, and you fucking hire him? What do you think that looks like to Singh now? Plus, who the fuck is he? We know nothing about him."

"Most of Singh's guys are terrified of him. The inspector told me how they all cowered in fear after he put six rounds in Adeepa. Though, I'm sure Singh and Lasal probably won't hesitate to go after him. But he was in town barely twenty minutes, and he killed one of them. The more I think about it, the only thing I think Singh might try next is to hire this guy for himself," James jeered.

"I don't fucking like it. I don't like sudden changes. And I don't like strange faces!"

I stood up. "You got a problem with me, then I suggest you talk it over with your leader here." I walked out of the kitchen toward the exit. I made sure to walk right by him and make eye contact as I left. Sonny gave me an irritable and untrusting look.

"Hey, wait. Where you going, John?" James called after me.

"Back to town."

"Wait, let me give you a ride."

"Nah, I'll walk." I needed to be alone, so I could think.

"Fuck him. Let him go," Sonny muttered.

I heard James starting to argue with Sonny as I got outside.

• • •

I walked along the dirt road. It would probably take me almost forty-five minutes to walk back to my car, but I needed to get the hell out of there. I didn't know who I was anymore. It was as if the real John Sandes had been taken over by some other entity.

"Goddamn James! And that prick Sonny. I could have walloped Sonny right there and then," I yelled to myself, took a deep breath of the air, and sighed. There was no time to fuck around. I had to develop a plan quickly. I tried to play it easy and cool, but it often backfired. My feelings were a roller coaster. Sometimes I'd feel entirely in control, and others like a madman possessed by a demon. It was as if I were a helpless passenger surrendering to the madness and rage. I was a ball of fury from witty and clever to a whirlwind of fire. That was the best name for it: the fury. Ever since my last case with the Seattle Police Department, I had started having visions of Mallory. They were beginning to become more and more frequent. That experience had ripped open a wound. Sometimes, I would get lost in the moment, forgetting Mallory wasn't there, but only in my imagination. Her voice had helped me on several occasions.

However, now I had crossed the line into something else entirely. I was straddling the boundary of being some rogue vigilante, tiptoeing into villainous territory. The longer I stuck around, the less I was afraid of these guys. James and Singh were nothing but a bunch of sorry thugs. But what I worried about most of all were the consequences down the road, acting the part of something I wasn't.

CHAPTER 8

As I returned to the other side of town, I found my car and checked to ensure everything was as I had left it. Everything seemed to be in order. There was no sign of the fuel attendant. I popped back into the unnamed restaurant—my spot. Despite being dangerously close to Singh and many other kooky characters, I felt comfort in this little establishment. Perhaps it was Calvin and his schoolboy attentiveness to me. He was a good kid. He was in his twenties, but his innocence made me think of him as a kid.

Nobody had seen me enter from the outside. As I walked in, I saw Calvin and a few other workers. In addition, there were three or four other patrons seated throughout various parts of the place.

"Oh. You're back," Calvin said. "I was worried something may have happened."

The rest of the employees and patrons stared at us.

"Still alive." I nodded at him. "Can I get some soup? Maybe coffee, too?"

"Of course." He darted off.

Several moments later, he returned with an unknown soup along with a cup of coffee. I took a small sip of the soup. It tasted like some kind of meat, possibly beef. Maybe just as well I didn't know what.

• • •

Thirty minutes later, I had finished the soup and was on my third cup of coffee. Deputy Inspectors Kanish and Khan walked in—Tweedledee and Tweedledum. They saw me immediately.

"Well, well, look who it is. The last time I talked with you, I advised you to get out of town. You had some altercation with Adeepa. Next thing I hear, he's dead," Khan said.

"Well, that conversation didn't go so well. Adeepa wasn't too talkative. But Kanish could probably relate to that. Isn't that right, Kanish?" I purposely looked in his direction to get a reaction out of him.

Both these guys were crooked as hell, but out of the two, I disliked Kanish more. Khan was a clown, but Kanish was too quiet for my liking. The quiet ones were always more dangerous.

"As I said before, Kanish doesn't talk much, but he listens pretty well. John, right? That's your name?"

It appeared my name was starting to get around. I nodded.

"What's your last name, John?"

"Funny, neither of you seemed to give a shit about me or what I had to say when I tried talking to you before." I took a long, loud slurp of my coffee in the most annoying way possible, then set the cup hard down on the table. Khan gave me an annoyed look. So, I did the only thing I could think of. I picked it up again and repeated, slurping until Kanish walked the hell off.

Khan stayed put. "You have a good day, John. I'm sure we will see you around." He nodded and walked away. I saw him join Kanish at a table in a separate part of the restaurant. Kanish was pissed. I would've loved to have popped him right in the mouth.

Calvin came over to me.

"Can I get you anything else, John?"

"Perhaps, yeah. Have a seat." I looked across the table at him. "I don't suppose there's a room attached to this joint you can rent me?"

"You know, I started to think maybe James had hired you, and you were going to be staying at the Kundali."

"Yeah, well. I'm not staying there. I only work for myself—no one else—I do what I want on my terms."

"I don't own the place, but I live upstairs, and there is an extra room. I'm sure the owner wouldn't mind. He's out of town for a while anyway, so I'm in charge here for the time being. I could use some extra money."

I reached into my pocket. "Okay, Calvin. You let me know when this runs out, and I'll give you some more," I said, handing him a thick stack of Sri Lankan rupees. It was probably the equivalent of around two hundred U.S. dollars. Still, I wasn't concerned about the cost of anything in this country. Everything was cheap enough.

"Oh, one more thing. I've been meaning to ask you about this. What's the deal with this woman that Adeepa poured acid on? What happened that made him do that?"

"That's his wife, Maleesha, or, I should say, his widow now. She was telling her female friends about Adeepa abusing her. He found out and didn't like that too much. Women need to be careful about going against men. She should've been more careful, to be honest."

"Adeepa was a piece of shit."

Calvin stayed silent. I stared around the room of people, who were all scared of Singh and James. As far as the inspectors were concerned, they also had their worries, which was me. They didn't fool me one bit, especially Kanish.

"Could you suggest the best way to approach Maleesha or some of her friends about what's going on here?"

His eyes got wide. "Ooh. I don't know about that. That will be tough. Even with Adeepa dead, she's on a tight leash. She's still in extreme pain. She went to a local hospital just outside of town, but now she's back down the street. I know exactly what building she stays in. She's being guarded by Singh's men, though, so it won't be easy to get to her."

"Does she have any family?"

"Her mother is deceased. From what I heard, her father sold her to Adeepa when she was just a teenager, or maybe it was an arranged marriage. It's hard to say. I only know what I hear from rumors. But I've never heard any other family mentioned."

"How old is she?" I asked.

"Oh, twenty-four or twenty-five, maybe."

"Adeepa was in his late thirties to early forties, right?"

Calvin nodded. "Yes, and they've been together at least eight or nine years."

I suddenly felt sick. The thought of women being sold by family members, and at such a young age. Despicable.

"Come to think of it, I do know some of her female friends who come in here regularly. They are also married to some of Singh's guys. Sometimes they come in together. Let me see what I can do. Give me a day or two," Calvin assured me.

I nodded at him.

CHAPTER 9

The last two days were surprisingly quiet. I had gotten settled in the room above the restaurant just down the hall from Calvin. My walks were only during daylight hours, and I was always armed, of course. I was still worried Singh was going to come after me. Calvin had told me what building Maleesha was in, and he had also gotten in touch with one of her girlfriends. She and her friend had agreed on a time and place to meet today and had given the meeting location to Calvin. It was decided that it was best to meet somewhere where we would not be seen together. One of Maleesha's friends had talked Singh into loosening his watch on her. He agreed to let her and her friend take a couple of hours a day to go on walks alone. They would use this time to meet with me.

• • •

I was about two miles away from the restaurant, just outside a large abandoned house that looked like it hadn't been lived in for ages. I had taken my vehicle this time. It was explicitly stated that I come alone, not that I had friends in this town anyway. I stared at my useless cell phone, using it solely as a clock. I was right on schedule, so Maleesha and her friend should be here. I stepped out of the car and approached the entrance. As I entered the house, a strong, musty odor hit me. Unlike the bright sunshine and sweltering heat outside, the inside was dark and chilly. Maybe I should hide out in here when I need to cool off. The lights were off, but I could still make out some human shapes.

"Hello, Mr. John," a female voice called out. "I'm sorry, I do not know your last name."

I didn't respond. There were two wooden chairs placed in the middle of the room, each with warm bodies sitting in them. I could not see any faces as they were obscured by the shadows. I stared at thin legs and shoes, quickly seeing they were both women.

"Please sit," the same voice said. She raised an arm out from the shadows and pointed at an identical empty chair sitting directly across from them. I sat down. A good dozen feet separated us from each other. I stared straight ahead in their direction, waiting for my eyes to fully adjust to the dark.

"Maleesha?" I called out softly.

"Yes," the voice on the right whispered.

"Let me see your face."

"No, I don't want anyone to see my face ever again."

The voice on the left spoke again. "She is grateful for what you did. Standing up for her like that was noble, but none of us women have many choices here. We are each risking our lives talking to you right now. We must serve Singh and his men and have no way to escape."

Maleesha spoke again. "Where are you from?"

"I'm from the US."

"Where exactly?"

"Lots of places."

"You are very skilled with the firearm."

"I've had lots of experience. I used to work for the police," I said, hoping that would help earn some trust.

"I see," the other woman said. "And what is it you want from us?"

"I can help you escape from here—from Singh. I can help you get out of the country. I know people who could help you. We could help each other out."

A faint creaking sounded from another part of the house. I froze. It was an old building, so it was probably expected. Perhaps I just heard things. After all, I wasn't getting any younger. My mind may not have been as sound as it used to be, but I'd hoped my hearing wasn't going as well.

"How exactly would you help us? What kind of information do you need from us?"

"I want all the dirt on everybody. All the crimes, drug trades, murders, acid attacks, anything you have. Listen, if—"

Loud footsteps came toward us from the back of the room. By instinct, I leaped out of my chair and dove away into the shadows beneath a nearby table. Shots hit the chair I had been sitting on seconds earlier. The wood on the backrest exploded. I had both guns drawn and fired four shots at the feet and legs of a man I could not see. He groaned, and I fired four more bullets into the shadows, trying to guess where his torso was positioned. As his body hit the ground, I quickly picked myself up just in time to see another man running inside from the main entrance. His gun was extended toward me, I fired two shots into his upper body, and he dropped hard to the floor. I spotted a light switch near the door and flipped it on. I was surprised to see the lights actually did work, and the room was illuminated. I wanted to kick myself for not doing that before. It would've saved me just a bit of trouble.

Both women were underneath a table on the far side of the wall. I pointed one gun in front of me while the other was aimed at the entrance door. I scanned every direction, waiting for more men to appear. I had gotten into the habit of counting my shots many years before, but occasionally I would miscount. I'd fired twelve, I thought. The two women got out from under the table, and I could clearly see that neither one of them was Maleesha. Both of them were perfectly intact with no deformities. Two dark-haired women, midtwenties to early thirties, with flawless faces. This was a setup! Everyone in this goddamn town was working against me. It felt like my head was on fire. The fury had returned, and I was losing control. I walked over to them, almost tripping over a chair and screaming in frustration as I banged my knee and kicked the chair clear across the other end of the room.

"Who are you two! Where's Maleesha! You set me up! Goddamn it! Now, tell me what the fuck is going on!" As I stormed toward them, I stopped just inches from their bodies. They were terrified as their eyes grew wide.

"We're sorry! We had no choice! Please! Please, don't hurt us! We were forced to do this," the girl who had been impersonating Maleesha said, starting to sob.

I took a step back. "What are your names? Your real names and no bullshit," I asked sternly.

"I'm Mali. I was told to pretend to be Maleeshi, and this is Tehani." She pointed at the other woman, who was speechless.

"How many more men were sent here to kill me?"

"It was just those two," Tehani said. "We were all supposed to contact Singh when the job was done. Calvin spoke to us yesterday when we walked into the restaurant. He wanted to keep things hush, but it was too late. One of Singh's men saw us and interrogated us shortly after. They told me if we didn't comply, they would hurt us the way they did Maleesha—or worse!"

I knew not to take being double-crossed personally. They were just trying to survive in a world where big fish eat little fish. The women in this town were always the little fish. They were nothing like my ex-wife, Samantha—she was a killer. She had once hired a hit man to take me out. But I was unable to prove it. I hadn't talked to her since, over two years ago.

"Go, get out of here." I made a motion, shooing them away.

"We don't want to go back there, but we don't have any other choice," Mali said, obviously shaken up. "Did you really mean what you said? Could you really help us get out of here?"

I looked outside to see if anyone else had shown up. Not a soul to be seen.

"Is there anything you need to go back for? Any personal possessions? Do you have children?" I asked them.

"We have nothing—no children. We have some clothing but nothing else to our name," Mali replied.

"Do you have anyone you can stay with who's far enough away from here and Singh—family members, friends?"

"My parents are deceased. I have no family except for a cousin in Point Pedro—up north. But I cannot afford to get there."

"Where's the nearest bus station?" I asked.

"About a thirty-minute drive from here," said Mali.

"Okay, I'll drive both of you and give you enough for a ride to Point Pedro. What do you say?"

They both nodded.

"My car is outside. Both of you get in the back seat, and lie down and stay out of sight."

• • •

The bus station was mostly empty, except for a few other people waiting. I bought two tickets to Point Pedro and handed them to the women. When the bus arrived, I asked the driver to guarantee the women got to their location. I handed him a stack of rupees, gave each of the women a stack, and asked if it was enough for them. They confirmed it was more than enough.

"By no circumstances, and I mean by none whatsoever, do you stray from this plan. You stay on this bus till you get dropped off at Point Pedro, then you go to your cousin. If you decide to do something else, then I can't help you any further."

They each nodded. I made sure they boarded the bus and watched as it drove off.

CHAPTER 10

I sat in my car, trying to think out my plan. I knew I could just drive out of here to another place and go on with my life. But what did I have to live for anyway? Once again, I felt that rage coming back inside me—the fury was at it again. I remember how I had felt when I had fought Larry. Goddamn him.

"Dad, you're going to get hurt if you're not careful. These guys don't mess around. You're getting too comfortable." Mallory's voice returned into my head.

I looked to my right, and there she was, sitting right in the passenger seat. I teared up as I saw her olive skin and dark hair. She looked exactly the way she had the last time I saw her, which was many years ago.

"I love you so much, baby." I turned the key in the ignition and pressed the gas. "But I have to finish this, or I won't be able to live with myself." I wiped my face with my sleeve, clearing away the tears before Mallory's apparition disappeared. No time for crying now. Gotta put on a good performance for all these shitheads.

• • •

I figured Singh would start to wonder what happened. I had been gone maybe two hours. To hell with it. I decided I would go directly to Singh's building. I guess it wouldn't be staffed with an entire crew, which would suit what I had planned. They most likely would've had a search party out looking for the two dead men who didn't return and the women I helped to escape.

I parked my car a couple of blocks away so no one would see or hear me pull up. I got to the building where I shot Adeepa. There was no one lurking around, and only one car parked outside. I circled the building, checking all the windows and doors. It was surrounded mostly by dirt, but there was a small patch of grass in the back with a white table and empty chairs. A bunch of cigarette butts in a glass ashtray sat on the table. A clothesline was tied between two trees with several articles of clothing left hanging.

Voices came from inside the house. I ran to the side of the building. I needed to get inside to see Maleesha, and this was my best shot at getting a proper conversation with her. I would try the back door and hope for the best. A moment later, a Sri Lankan woman came out, carrying a basket of wet clothing. She was of medium height, around five-five, dark hair, medium-tan complexion, looked to be in her early thirties. I had never seen this woman before. She hung several items along the clothesline, using two clothespins to secure each thing.

Clearly, I hadn't thought this through well enough. Once again, I did not know what I was supposed to do, but now it was time to make a move, whatever that was. Shit. Okay, I had an idea—kind of a stupid one, but I'd try it.

"Meow, meow, meow." I did my best to imitate the sound of a cat. I hadn't seen any cats around, but what the hell. There had to be some cats around here. Or, maybe there weren't cats here, and then it would *definitely* get someone's attention.

I peered around the corner to see the woman turn in my direction. "Meow! Meow!" I called again, increasing my voice. I ran to the front of the house, continued over to the other side, and came around the opposite way returning to the backyard. I was just in time to see the woman walking in the direction of the side I had just been thirty seconds earlier. I snuck up from behind, grabbed her, and placed my hand over her mouth. I faintly heard her start to scream.

"Shhh. I'm not going to hurt you. My name is John. It was me who killed Adeepa." I spun her around so she could see me. I took my hand off her mouth. "Please. I just want to talk to you."

"You? You're the foreigner they were after. They sent men to kill you," she said as she gave me a wide-eyed look.

"How is Maleesha? I was there when they splashed acid in her face."

"She is in terrible shape. She is blind. The doctor doesn't think she will ever be able to see again. She barely moves, speaks, or eats. The life has been sucked out of her. She has said she wishes she had died."

"Who are you?"

"Saanvi."

"Are you friends with Maleesha?"

"Yes, I mean, we have bonded. Women must stick together here. We have to look out for each other. I was sold to my husband many years ago by my father in exchange for money. I grew up in a small village several hours north of here. My husband works for Singh."

"Jesus, I'm sorry."

She shrugged. "It's life."

"Who else is in the house?"

"Maleesha and I are here alone. Singh was expecting to hear back from his men that he sent to kill you, but they never returned. Everyone left except for the two of us and my husband, who went to talk to the inspectors. You should leave before he gets back, which I expect will be soon."

"I need to see Maleesha first. Can you take me to see her, please?"

"But if my husband returns and sees you—"

"I have to try. Please," I pleaded with her.

She nodded and led me inside the house through the back entrance. The three-story house was relatively spacious. Saanvi led the way up the stairs and down to the far end of the hallway. We stepped into a large room with an empty bed. The curtains were closed, and the light was not very bright. I looked around, confused, unable to see anyone else in the room. Saanvi turned to me and pointed to a small staircase leading up to the attic.

"She stays up here. This is Adeepa's old room, but he usually makes her stay up there." She pointed up to the attic. "Since the acid attack, she only leaves to use the bathroom. I have to constantly remind her to eat now. She doesn't do hardly anything." Hearing her describe Maleesha's state burned my blood. I thought of Mallory. If someone had hurt my daughter like this, I swear to Christ. Damn it, I needed to focus and reminded myself that I was in Sri Lanka and not the US. Mallory wasn't here. It was Maleesha.

Saanvi stopped before the top of the stairs and called out softly, "Maleesha?"

We heard a faint groan from the attic.

"I just want to rest, please," we heard Maleesha say.

"The man who killed Adeepa is here. He wants to talk with you."

There was a moment of silence. I waited, trying to be patient, but I wanted to run up there.

"Come in," she finally responded.

Saanvi waved her hand for me to approach. I got to the top of the steps and entered the attic with Saanvi right behind me.

CHAPTER 11

Straight ahead, I saw a woman in a headscarf sitting on a small mattress on the floor. Several bottles and containers of medical supplies were near her—assortments of bandages, lubricants, gels, liquids, and tablets. I approached her.

"Stop." She raised her hand. "Please, don't come any closer."

I stopped, respecting her wishes.

"Maleesha, my name is John. You don't know me, but—"

"You killed Adeepa," she interrupted me.

I paused.

"I was just passing through when I saw you come out of the restaurant. I'm sorry about what happened. I can't imagine what type of pain this has caused you. Nobody should ever have to endure something like that. It's inhumane. Not just the acid attack, but everything else these men have done to you. I heard you were just a teenager when your father sold you to Adeepa. There's nothing I can do to undo the suffering you have experienced. I want to help you."

Maleesha burst into tears. I walked over and knelt in front of her, wrapping my arms around her. As she rested her head on my shoulder, she cried. Her tears dripped onto my skin, causing my heart to break and think of

Mallory. A long time passed as we embraced each other. She finally raised her head and removed her headscarf so I could see her face. Her mangled head barely resembled anything human. My gaze rested on the disfigured face, the skin tissue of which looked damaged beyond repair. It was a horrific sight to see the physical scars. Still, I couldn't imagine what it must have been like for her to go through the psychological and emotional pain. She would indeed feel immense anxiety and depression for a long time.

I looked at her face and saw a poor innocent soul who deserved to live. She had human rights. She had a right to not have acid thrown in her face. She had a right to not be sold by her father as a child to some man she barely knew, a man who would torment and abuse her.

"A real man would do this to no one. A real father would not do this to his daughter. A real husband would not do this to his wife," I whispered.

"Do you have a daughter, John?"

"Yes, but she doesn't talk to me anymore."

"I find that hard to believe. I can't see you, but I can tell from your voice and your energy that you are a good man."

"Perhaps, but I've made mistakes in the past. I have to pay for those mistakes. I want to make them right." I was getting choked up. Maleesha put her hand on my face.

"Let me get you both out of here," I said.

"No, I'm in no condition to go anywhere. I'm in too much pain, but there is one thing you can do for me, John."

"What is that? Anything."

She leaned in close and whispered into my ear, "Make them all pay." She grabbed me tight. "I have nothing else to live for. If I could know these men would pay . . . it . . . it would give me the will to go on a little longer. I want to die, John."

"Don't kill yourself, Maleesha."

"If you promise to make them pay, I promise I won't kill myself—for now. Don't tell Saanvi I said that to you." Then she crawled away from me and lay back down.

I turned to see Saanvi still standing near the foot of the stairs. I walked back over to her and said, "I'm ready to go now."

"Yes, it's a good idea. My husband will be home soon."

We had just gotten down to the ground floor when the door opened. A fat man—late forties, about five-nine—strolled inside. He saw both of us. His face carried a shocked expression that turned quickly to anger.

"What the fuck, woman! Who the fuck do you think you are?" he growled at each of us. This was obviously the charming husband. Another winner.

He charged right up to me and got inches from my face. "You're dead, you son of a—"

I pushed him away. As he charged at me again, I punched him right in the face, knocking his fat frame and fat ass out cold. His body hit the side of a wall, knocking down an array of items along with it and nearby shelves, including liquor bottles, small boxes, hammers, and various other tools. Saanvi stared in horror. I walked over to him and rested my hand on his fat face.

"I can feel a large lump here. He will be out a while. When he comes to, tell him I forced myself in here. If he even remembers anything." As I exited the front door, I turned to face her and said, "When this is all over, I'll be back."

CHAPTER 12

I arrived at the Kundali, parked the car, and stepped out. I walked into the hotel, past a few guys. James and about seven or eight others were talking inside the lobby. When he saw me, he looked over.

"Where have you been, John?"

"I killed two more of Singh's guys."

Sonny stood up. "Really? Is that bullshit or what?"

James got up and put his hand on Sonny's shoulder to calm him.

"I tried to organize a meeting with Maleesha in secret, but it was a setup." I left out the part about going back to Singh's building.

"Well, what did you expect? You can't trust a man like Singh or anyone who is associated with him, no matter who they are," James responded.

"I shot them both on the spot."

"Jesus fucking Christ!" Sonny shouted.

"Sonny, calm down. John, want a drink?"

"Scotch on the rocks," I said.

James motioned to one of his men to mix the drink. A moment later, he handed it to me.

"So, there's something I'd like—" James was interrupted by a loud crash from a nearby room.

One of his men came out into the lobby a moment later. "James! It's the kid! Get over here quick!"

James and everyone else ran, stopping outside the door to the room. It was a lounge with a large sofa, two oversized cushy chairs, a wooden coffee table, and a large flat-screen TV mounted to the wall. The kid I'd watched get shot up on heroin the other night was on the sofa. His eyes were closed, and he was foaming at the mouth. His body was convulsing.

"What the fuck happened?" James turned to the man.

"I don't know. The kid was testing some of the goods, and it happened suddenly. I've never seen him like this before," he answered.

Suddenly, the kid stopped moving. Saliva ran down his mouth and onto his ragged shirt. James grabbed his arm to feel for a pulse and placed his hand over his heart. He lifted the kid's scrawny little arm to the air and released, letting it drop lifelessly against the sofa.

"This kid is fucking dead. Goddammit." James was pissed. "Now we have to find a new tester."

My gaze was filled with disgust watching these people who cared little about human life. They were heartless and cruel.

"Pick him up and get him the hell out of here," James scolded the man.

"Where should I take him, boss?"

"Here, follow me." James gestured to him as the man carried all ninety pounds of the kid's limp body. We followed them. They went out through the main entrance with James leading the way. James walked about one hundred paces from the property and pointed at the ground.

"Throw his ass right here. The crows can eat him for all I care. He's got no family. No one is gonna come looking for him."

The man walked to where James was standing and threw the body down. It made a loud crunching sound on the dirt. I saw Lana from the corner of my eye—gazing at the still body of the boy. God damn these people. God damn them all. The fury was inside me once again. James and everyone came back into the hotel. I didn't know how much more of this shit I could take. I had to hold back the anger and keep a cool head. As I got back inside, I walked over to where I had set my glass of scotch and picked it up.

"It's a great thing you work for us," James said. It was as if none of the last several minutes had even happened. "Remember, we've got that big shipment of heroin coming in tomorrow night. That one I told you about. I'll repeat it again—I'd like you there with us. I'm sure Singh is pretty pissed with the way you've been cutting away at his employees. They might try to intercept our shipment now that you're on our side. I'll give you a nice cut of the profits." He smiled.

He expected me to say yes.

At first, I had considered hanging out here a little longer to extract some more helpful information, but seeing that stunt with the kid had ruined my mood. I took one long, slow sip of the scotch until it was all gone.

"I'll think about it," I said before turning my back to walk out.

"What are you holding out for, John? It would be a mistake to not accept the offer," James called out.

"Show some respect!" Sonny snapped. "Don't turn your back on us like that. Don't let him fucking walk away! You let him walk away?" He looked at James. "No, fuck that! Nobody pulls that shit on us."

I'd just gotten outside the door when I felt Sonny's hand grab the back of my neck.

"You get back here, you son of a bitch!"

The sharp pain of fury in my head intensified as I felt his hand. As I spun around, I grabbed him by both arms and threw him down the steps into the dirt. I hopped down onto the ground, stood over him, and kicked him in the stomach.

"What? You got something to say? Goddamn punk! Huh? What did you call me? Son of a bitch? Is that right? Who's the bitch now?" I bent over and punched him several times in the face. Several guys drew their guns, but James waved them off.

"Put the guns down." He motioned to his men.

I repeatedly hit Sonny until he stopped moving. Suddenly there were other visitors in my mind.

"Ol' man. You can't win this one." Larry's voice had entered my head. "Give up now."

"I whooped you pretty good, and you couldn't catch me, could ya?" Marlboro Man's voice echoed.

"It's Mallory or me. You must choose," Samantha spoke.

"Fuck you! Fuck all of you! You goddamn bastards! Fuck! Fuck! Spineless bastard cunts!" I wanted to take them all on.

"Dad, save me. Don't leave me. Please! Don't you love me?" Mallory cried.

"I did the best I could! I did my best to be a good father. You are so dear to me. I tried to find you, Mallory, but you disappeared. You left! I'm so sorry. I failed you as a father!" I screamed.

CHAPTER 13

JAMES/AUSSIES

James stared in shock at John's breakdown, not knowing what to make of it. He was perturbed but also fascinated.

"Holy shit! This guy's a complete lunatic," Jim said. "Should we shoot him right here, boss?"

"No. No. Put that damn thing down. Just cool it for a minute, will you?"

"I did everything I could! Why, Samantha? Why did you do this to me?" John continued. "Why did you do this to me? You hired someone to have me killed! Goddamn bitch!" John was simultaneously screaming and bawling. "Marlboro Man! Where are ya? Stop hiding! I'll finish you when I find you!"

Suddenly, from out of nowhere, his whole persona transformed itself yet again. "*You little shit! What the fuck did you do today, Johnny? I heard you caused trouble at Catholic school. I heard the nuns beat the shit out of you! Come here, boy! Papa is gonna thump you really good! Get yer ass over here now, goddammit!*"

John's voice was completely different—his pitch and tone—as if possessed by someone else. He pulled both guns out and aimed at the sky, still angrily muttering words that made no sense whatsoever.

Sonny remained still on the ground, baffled at what he saw. When he finally picked himself up, he ran over to James.

"Let's shoot this fucker right now!" He brought his gun up and aimed at John.

"No!" James snatched the gun out of his hand. "He might still be of use to us. He's crazy for sure. A real loose cannon, but I like our chances against Singh with this guy around. Just stand back."

John's screams halted, and his voice became softer. His speech returned to normal. "What have I done? Where have I gone wrong? Why me? I have to make things right. I will find you, Mallory, I promise."

Lana stood behind everyone else, watching the mysterious stranger, and felt sorry for him. The last time he had visited, she had not realized the man's complexity. She thought John was just another man wanting to make some money. He was in pain and not well. She now understood there was much more to him than what was on the surface. She felt an attraction to him as a daughter would with her father.

CHAPTER 14

I had forgotten what had happened in the last few moments. I remembered beating the shit out of Sonny, but the next thing I knew, I had Larry and Mallory on my mind, with both guns in my hands. I didn't remember pulling them out. Strange—a momentary blackout. I knew sometimes I would get worked up when pushed, but it had been a while since I last blacked out. I stared at James and his men. Sonny, somehow, was magically standing with them. I quickly recomposed myself.

"I don't like being fucked with. You guys wanna tussle? I don't give a shit. I'm ready to die. I'll go down swingin'. You don't believe me—try me," I said forcefully.

"Calm down, John. I get it. Sorry about Sonny here. He's a hothead, and he should know better." He gave Sonny a hard stare. "You do what you want. I got it. Take some time to think things over. You'll be back, I'm sure of it." James smiled and waved.

Once I realized James and his men weren't going to further retaliate, I holstered my guns. I caught a glimpse of Lana—she was staring at me from behind the other men. I wanted to talk with her, but my mood had been soured—another time, maybe. I got into my car and drove back to the other side of town.

• • •

Once I arrived back at the restaurant, Calvin gave me the rundown of what had happened since my departure. When Singh had not heard back from either of the women or his two thugs he had sent to kill me, he had gone to investigate. When he saw the bodies and no signs of the women or me, he reported it to the crooked lawmen. Khan and Kanish showed up shortly after to poke around. They were probably disappointed I hadn't been slaughtered. I was still a problem in their eyes. Nobody had heard anything after that. I was sure getting under the skin of a lot of people here.

"John, I'm sorry about what happened. I had no idea it was a setup, I swear. I would never do that. I didn't know. I was just trying to do what you—"

"Calvin, it's okay. I believe you. Guess what? I did get to talk to Maleesha. After I shot those guys, I headed over to Singh's building. I figured they'd be looking for me when his guys didn't come back." I grinned.

"Holy shit. You knew the house would be unguarded, didn't you? That was a hell of a move, sir. You're like a detective of some sort." He smiled.

I smiled back. "Of a sort. Singh will think twice before pulling any stunts with me from now on," I continued, showing confidence I hoped wouldn't make me careless in the future.

"Would you like a scotch on the rocks?" he asked.

"No, just a glass of water. Actually, I'll take another steak too."

"We have some local Sri Lankan food, as well."

"Another time. I'll go with the steak for now."

"Two more of Singh's guys added to your tally," Calvin said with a smile on his face.

"What the hell are you beaming about?"

"I'm just happy to see someone finally stand up to those thugs once and for all. So, are you working for James or not?"

I shrugged as he set the cutlery down in front of me. I examined the slightly dirty utensils and said, "These are grubby."

Calvin snatched them from my hands and quickly returned with a clean set.

I felt like this whole little game I was playing would soon come to an abrupt end. I may have looked self-assured and shown resolve, but the truth was I was running out of tricks. I didn't want to slip up, which meant I needed to ease up on the booze. At my age, I had to be extra careful. Another fifteen minutes or so went by, and my steak was finally ready. Calvin came out with the sizzling plate and set it in front of me. I cut into it and took a small bite. I looked up just in time to spot a dark, slender man, maybe midforties, walking into the restaurant with four other men on their high horse—or horses.

"Sitting out here unprotected isn't very wise," he said as he and his party looked at me with serious expressions.

I stood up, pulling out my guns, even if I knew I was outmatched. The four men aimed their pistols directly at me while the slender man remained unfazed, staring at me inquisitively.

"What's the deal? I figured everyone liked me 'cause I'm such a popular guy." I gave a smirk, continuing to add to my calm façade.

Trying to appear cute and cool became increasingly infuriating for me as time went on. It was challenging to appear unruffled, as I was irritable. Despite my best efforts to convince everyone I was always ten steps ahead, in truth, I was much further behind. If people knew that, then they could use it to my disadvantage.

I guessed who this guy was instantly, and, truthfully, I wanted to strangle him. *Keep your cool, John. Keep your cool. Breathe.*

"I'm gonna guess you're Mr. Singh."

"Bingo, give this man a million dollars!" He smiled devilishly.

"We can keep doing this back-and-forth bullshit, but I'm not afraid to go down guns blazing. I'm sure I can take one of you down with me."

He let out a sleazy laugh. "Relax, and let's talk."

I re-holstered both my weapons and sat back down. There wasn't going to be any shooting, at least not yet.

"Mind if I have a seat?" He didn't wait for me to answer before sitting down, not that he had to.

"So you're not gonna kill me right here?"

"Kill you? Ha! Well, I've tried that already, and we see how that's worked out. Now you kind of intrigue me, John. That's your name, right? Forgive me. I don't know your last name."

I didn't respond and just kept my gaze on him.

"So, those two women I sent to talk with you. They've disappeared."

"Is that right?" I responded nonchalantly.

One of the men lunged forward at the table. "You son of a bitch! Where is Mali? That's my girl!" He put his hands on me, and I threw him onto the floor.

The other three men took a few steps toward me. Singh finally stood up to face his men and barked, "Enough." He turned back toward me. "Make no mistake, there will be consequences if we find out you had anything to do with their disappearance."

I shrugged, changing the subject. "So what's your business exactly? Are you into drug trafficking like James?"

He chuckled. "Oh, I'm in a lot of industries. James thinks he's hot shit, but he's as vanilla as they come. He's pretty clean and green if you ask me."

"Nobody in this town is clean or green."

"Ha. Yeah? Well, you sure as hell aren't either. I can tell just by looking at you. You're a damaged man, John, or whatever the hell your name is. I've seen others like you. You try to fool everyone around you, but the truth is you're only fooling yourself."

"You know nothing about me."

"Well, for one, you parade around the place acting like you're some twenty-something-year-old action hero. Yeah, you're tough, but you're an old man. You don't have much time left. You're wearing down." He smiled as he pulled a cigar and match from his pocket. He lit the cigar and took a deep puff, blowing out the smoke toward me.

His crack about my age had annoyed me—not that it wasn't true—but there's only one person I allow to make cracks about my age—me.

"So, you deal drugs and abuse women. That's your legacy."

He snickered. "You think I'm some small-time hood?"

I honestly wasn't quite sure what to think, but either I was right or wrong. Regardless, Singh would tell me his game, and I would listen, whether I wanted to or not.

"Do you remember the Mumbai bombings last year?"

I nodded.

"That was my doing."

"How so? The people behind that were from Pakistan. You're lying."

He gave out a fiendish shriek. "Oh, am I?"

"Why would you—"

"I had men helping them. I supplied them with weapons, money, and valuable information. Where to go, when, who to target, where the weak points were. You know, all the details. The Pakistanis pay well. What can I say?" He shrugged as if it were nothing.

This guy was total garbage. I was ready to start swinging if need be. But I still wanted to extract more information. "Back to you and James?" I asked.

"We've had lots of problems in the past, and we still do," Singh continued. "Right now, we have an agreement to not meddle in each other's affairs. He has cost me serious money, and money lost is a concern. I can't prove it, but I know he was behind one of our stolen drug shipments a while back. He's a cocksucker."

No disagreement from me there. It takes one to know one.

"He has a big shipment coming in at a port near Dondra tomorrow," I explained, figuring this would be the perfect time to pit Singh and James against each other.

"Is that right? Dondra? I know that port," Singh answered, deeply curious.

"That's what I heard. Maybe now is the right time to hit back." I smiled at the thought of Singh and James eliminating each other.

"He told you about this shipment? Aren't you working for him now?"

"Nah, I don't work for anyone but myself. Besides, I had a little scuffle with one of James's goons earlier today. Sonny."

Singh roared with laughter, followed by chuckles from his men. "Is that right? Holy shit, you're a character, all right. Perhaps you could prove useful to us."

The four men stared in disbelief. The man who had yelled before opened his mouth again. "You mean we're not going to waste this asshole, boss?" The other men nodded and agreed in unison. They were ready for a fight, and so was I. I might even be able to shoot two of them before they got a shot in.

"No, leave him be for now," Singh told them, without looking away from me. "I wouldn't get too comfortable if I were you."

"That's kinda hard, seeing as this town is so hospitable." I grinned. I could tell that comment had pissed him off.

He responded with a diabolic smile of his own. "We'll be in touch, John. Let's go, boys." He turned around, and his men followed him out the door.

Calvin, who'd been watching the entire exchange, came over to me as soon as Singh was out the door. "You think you could take on the rest of all these guys if it came down to it?"

I shrugged. "Maybe. I'm as healthy as a horse," I said, shoving another bite of my steak into my mouth.

"What's the deal with you and horses?"

I gave him a bamboozled look.

"First, you want to eat one of them, and now you're comparing your health to one?"

I chuckled. "Figures of speech is all. Don't overthink things."

Needing to contemplate the Singh and James situations, I shooed Calvin away. Singh didn't trust me—that much was clear. He would try to use me against James. James would try to use me against Singh. I would use them against each other. Everyone in this town was getting used one way or another.

CHAPTER 15

I woke up early Saturday morning and decided to get out of Dodge for the day. I didn't want anyone finding me—James or Singh. I'm sure James would send some of his men to come find me for help with the shipment later that night, but I had no intention of going. I didn't want to be anywhere nearby. I wanted to see how things would play out between the two rivals. I drove about an hour north inland and walked around gathering my thoughts.

"Do you think this plan will work, Dad?"

"I don't know, but I don't have a lot of options. These guys are well connected. I'm fairly certain they've bribed all the law enforcement inside the country."

"Eventually, Singh and James will catch on."

"I have no doubt."

"Maleesha's entire life ruined in one instant when that acid splashed her face."

"It was ruined long before that, Mallory. Long before."

"That poor kid overdosed at the Kundali. They threw his body onto the dirt like he was worthless."

"These people are all goddamn bastards. Each and every one. This place is soulless and evil. It's like all the bad energy gets absorbed in it. Sure, I could run away, but your demons follow you when you run away. I'm destined to experience the consequences of my past mistakes, constantly haunted by them without ever escaping. At the very least, I should do the best I can. This is not about me. It's not my story. It's about the fight!"

"The fight?"

"Yes!"

I screamed, realizing I had been talking to my imaginary daughter. My real daughter was out there somewhere. I tried to snap back into the moment, but the thought of all these evil people around me ignited that fury again. Fuck. I couldn't deal. I felt light-headed and collapsed onto the ground. As my mind whirled with all these thoughts, I closed my eyes. I felt as if my body had gone numb and into a deep meditative state.

CHAPTER 16

John Sandes knelt down on the dirt ground. The area was deserted—not a single human for miles. His mind was not here, but elsewhere, as if someone had just flipped an OFF switch. He remained silent and stagnant, his brain rebooting like a computer. A moment later, his eyes opened wide. He contorted his face into a furious rage.

In silence, he gazed out at nothing. After a moment, he started muttering angrily under his breath. It gradually got louder. He rose to his feet and began to stutter, "J-J . . . Johnny. J-John-ny." His body movement and facial expression changed. Everything about him was different. He was no longer John Sandes but someone else entirely. He soon exploded in screams.

"Johnny! Come here! You little bastard. Where are you? You didn't do all your chores. I beat your older brother. Now it's your turn. Come on out! I said come out! Don't you hide from me, boy. Take it like a man, Johnny. You're not a man, are ya? Ha ha! I didn't want two sons. Did I ever tell ya that, boy? I never wanted sons. You know why that is? I always favored your niece over you and your brother! Because girls can at least fulfill certain nee—"

CHAPTER 17

I woke up lying in the dirt. Had I dozed off in the middle of the afternoon? I hadn't realized how tired I was. I tilted my head to the sun. After brushing the dirt off my body, I stood up slowly. I should see a doctor about the blackouts, but that would have to wait. My mind wandered back to Maleesha and what she had said to me: "Make them all pay." Then I thought of Lana, her being with James, in his bed, lying next to him, his dirty hands on her . . .

Goddammit, John, focus! What the hell was wrong with me? Once again, I found myself asking why I was involved in all of this mess. What business did I have here anyway? What was the point of it all? Was it because I was a nice guy? A crazy guy? A good guy? A careless guy? Perhaps all of those things—or maybe none. I only knew one thing. The more James and Singh fought against each other, the easier it would be for me in the end. Let them kill each other first, then see who's left to deal with and go from there. I walked around for the rest of the day, going nowhere in particular and returning to my vehicle just before sunset. I sat in the back seat, drinking a large water bottle and reflecting on my life per my usual habit.

• • •

March 2007

I was a bloody mess. I had heard the man enter my apartment—I was a light sleeper. It was a struggle, though a short one. It had been my habit to keep a gun next to me for as long as I can remember, but over the last couple of years, I kept one even closer, underneath a pillow. The situation had remained unchanged since my previous case with the Seattle Police. When the man had raised his gun, I shot him in the chest. It was dark, and it was the best shot I could get off. It wasn't a lethal shot. I asked him why he had come after me. He didn't try to hide that my ex-wife, Samantha, had hired him. As I was calling the police, he knocked my gun out of my hand. After making his escape, rather than finishing the job, he left a trail of blood all over my apartment. Needless to say, I moved out after the incident. The police arrived, and I gave them my story. My old pal Clay Parker, a crime analyst from Forensics, came by to test for fingerprints and analyze blood samples, hoping they could identify the mysterious man. They never did. He got away scot-free.

The next day I made a telephone call, but not to Samantha. I called her first ex-husband, Dan. I hadn't talked to this guy in probably over thirty years. I had no reason to. He had only been married to Samantha for three years, escaping mainly unscathed. Basically, a starter marriage for both of them. I got to deal with all the crazy shit.

Dan had once mentioned that Samantha did something early on in their marriage, something that had seriously disturbed him, but he would never say what. The guy lived in Long Island, New York. To my knowledge, he still lived in the same place. I confirmed this by doing some Google searches, finding the information and phone number matching what I'd written down in an old address book. I punched in his number on my cell phone.

"Hello?"

"Hello, Dan, it's John Sandes."

"Um, oh. Hello, John. What do I owe the pleasure?" he said with a surprised tone.

"How are you feeling these days?"

"Oh, you know how it is as we get older. The parts don't work quite as well anymore, but I'm still functioning okay. Miss being in my twenties, though."

"I know that feeling," I replied. Dan was close to the same age—just a few years older, in his early seventies.

"Look, I'll just get straight to the point. A man made an attempt on my life last night. He said Samantha hired him to do it."

"Oh my God. Are you sure, John? I mean, you're sure she would really do that? Surely not."

"It amazes me how many people are still fooled by her. She's a pathological liar. We know she can easily pass lie detector tests, and she's been mentally unstable since she was a young girl. I'm an ex–police detective. Why would you still be in her corner after everything?"

"Look, John, I'm not taking her side. I'm just saying that's a big deal. Accusing your ex-wife of attempted murder—"

"I know she did it; I know. Tell me what she did when you were married to her."

"What are you talking—"

"That thing you've talked about but won't say what it is. Tell me!"

"Look, that was a long time—"

"Dan, just cut the horseshit, okay? Just fucking say it. Did she kill someone? Did she poison someone? Did she kill an animal? Did she abuse someone? Did she hurt someone? What?"

"Goddammit, John, leave it alone! It's been over forty years since I was married to her. Why are you calling me after all these years, stirring the pot?"

"I just told you that our ex-wife hired a hit man to take me out! I saw him with my own eyes, and he told me. Based on what we know about her past, do you think I'm lying? Seriously, what the fuck is wrong with you, Dan? Get your goddamn head outta yer ass and be a man!"

"Fuck you, John. And don't call me again."

I heard the phone slam down onto the receiver from his end.

Well, fuck, that went well.

• • •

It would have been nice to have lived a simpler life, but that would have been dull. My life certainly may not have been the best, but, at least, it was interesting. I took another long swig of water and drifted off to sleep. Tomorrow would be another long day.

CHAPTER 18

SONNY/AUSSIES

Shortly before sunset, Sonny arrived at the port near Dondra along with seven other men in various vehicles. He glanced around and could see the Dondra Lighthouse in the faint distance, a place nobody visited anymore. The light hadn't been used there in many years. He and his men waited patiently at the drop-off point for the boat to arrive with the goods. About thirty minutes later, it got dark. The only visible light was from their vehicle headlights.

A trawler boat appeared on the water heading their way. As it got closer, they could see two men were on board in addition to the captain. The men were white guys—Australians. Sonny could see both of them stacking the boxes. There should've been ten containers in total, two for each vehicle. The trawler docked at the pier. As the men, including the captain, were about to start unloading the boxes down the ramp, Sonny heard several cars pull up behind him.

"Hold it right there!"

Singh exited his vehicle.

"Holy shit!"

Sonny saw Singh had brought his entire posse. At least a dozen cars. There were three times as many of them as he and his guys.

"Leave the drugs on the boat, please," Singh said calmly.

"No! No, you're not taking our shipment!" Sonny yelled, taking a few steps toward Singh.

Singh turned around, gestured to his men, and they pointed their weapons at the boat. Shots were fired at the trawler, hitting all three men. Sonny and his guys dropped to the ground, raising their hands up. To Sonny, it felt as if the shooting lasted for minutes, but, in reality, it was about fifteen seconds. The three bodies were full of bullet holes, and blood covered the ramp where they had been standing. A few of the boxes had gotten hit as well, but most were intact, and their product had not suffered. One of Singh's men boarded the ramp and kicked the bodies into the water, each making a large splash as their dead weight hit the surface.

"What the fuck! We have a cease-fire!"

"Fuck you, Sonny." Singh stood over him. "I know you guys stole our shipment, and now you hire this John guy to fuck with us!"

"I don't like him either. It wasn't my choice, not my decision," he said, cowering in fear.

"Yea, well, you tell James that these are the consequences of his actions and poor decision-making. That foreigner has killed three of my guys so far. Three! Adeepa was one of my best shooters."

"Okay, take the shipment. Fine, just take it all. Just don't hurt us, please."

Singh pointed his firearm at one of Sonny's men down on the ground. Shots fired into the head of the man, and his body violently shook before going forever silent.

"No!" Sonny screamed.

"That's one." Singh smiled calmly. "And, let's see, who else? Maybe you, Sonny?"

"No! Please! I'll do whatever you want."

Singh looked around and pointed at another of Sonny's men. "Shoot him."

The man tried to protest. "No—" It was too late. The man's brains splattered onto the ground, his lifeless body falling facedown.

"Oh, got to make it even now. Three of our guys are dead, so we need to make it three for you, right? Fair is fair, and I'm not counting the boatmen." Singh pointed at the man right next to Sonny, and shots were fired into him.

Sonny closed his eyes and shook with fear as some of the man's blood sprayed onto his clothing and face.

"Now, we are taking this boat along with your drugs. You can tell your boss that if he doesn't watch his step, you will all be dead next time." Singh laughed at the sight of Sonny pleading for his life. "What a fucking coward you are, Sonny."

A few of Singh's men boarded the boat and took it away, while Singh and the rest got back into their cars and drove off.

Sonny screamed, "Fuck!"

Ever since that damned American had been in town, the shit had hit the fan. He was sure none of this would've been happening if it weren't for him. He wasn't sure who he wanted to kill more—Singh or John.

Sonny and his remaining men left the port, heading back to the Kundali to tell James what had happened.

CHAPTER 19

Sunday morning, I woke up and drove around a bit. The weather was hot, and I was tired. I spotted a food stand in the middle of nowhere and got some grub and coffee. The seller said I was his first customer in two days and was happy to see me. I handed him a few bills of paper and asked him if it was enough; it was equivalent to about two U.S. dollars. He nodded in agreement. I had stopped trying to count the funny money. I had no worries at all in regard to cash. The only problem was everything else. I hadn't even asked what the food was, but only one dish was available. The man gave me a small paper bowl and fork. I stared at the food and poked at it.

"Fish?"

The street vendor nodded his head. "Yes. Fish curry. Rice and vegetables. Very good."

I asked him for a water bottle, too, giving him another bill. I nodded and thanked him as he handed it to me. I sat in my car, the door open, my legs facing sideways. I was savoring the food. This was good stuff. I should try to have more of the local food. I finished eating, placing the trash on the passenger floor in my vehicle. I hung around the area for another couple of hours, walking around for some exercise and burning off some calories. Finally, I got back into my car and stared at myself in the rearview.

My hair was almost entirely gray around the sides and bald on top. For years, I had kept one side of it grown out long, simply brushing it over the top before finally cutting it and accepting the fact there wasn't anything up there.

"Christ," I muttered.

I reached into the back seat and grabbed my madras hat. I turned the key and drove off. Bringing my mind back to the business at hand, I was sure when I got back into town I'd hear about some shit that went down last night.

• • •

I rolled back into Mehliana right around noon. One of my tires had gone flat, and it took me a little longer than I'd anticipated. Luckily, I hadn't gone too far out. I drove right by a bunch of Singh's men. They stared at me, and I stared back, snickering to myself before parking in front of the fuel station. I went over to the fuel attendant.

"Hi there. I wondered if you or anyone you know could set me up with a spare. My tire is flat. It's not driving very well," I said.

The man looked at me. "Yeah, you're that foreigner who's been the talk of the town lately. Yes, I can help you. I'm also a mechanic and can fix that flat for you. It will be cheaper if I just repair it. Give me a day or two, okay?"

"Sure thing, much obliged. I'm staying right next door, so just come find me when you need to and let me know what I owe you." I smiled, both of us nodding in agreement with each other, and I walked off.

I went into the restaurant. It was the most crowded I had seen it yet. Calvin was serving a table of three. Three other workers on shift were serving customers at various tables. Inspector Khan was back, too, seated at a table by himself. I walked over and sat down at the table right next to him.

"Fancy seeing you here again." I smiled.

"You know there's been a whole hell of a lot of commotion since you came into this town. If I didn't know better, I'd say you're the cause of it."

"Is that right?"

"Uh-huh. Last night, I heard an altercation between Singh and some of James's men happened not far from here. Surprised you weren't there. Where have you been, anyway?"

I'm sure Khan knew the details and was fishing for information about my intentions.

"Oh, I decided to do some sightseeing. You know me, nothing but a simple tourist. Couldn't hurt a fly," I said.

Khan gave an amused chuckle. "Yeah. Uh-huh."

I called Calvin over to order some food. This time I picked a local curry dish, similar to what I had just ordered hours earlier. I was eager to compare the quality of the two. It took much less time to prepare than the steak. The food was ready in less than five minutes. It was gone in a flash as I was hungry despite having already eaten from that food stand earlier.

Calvin came over again. "How was it? Did you like the local curry dish?"

"It was damn good, sir. I needed the fuel to keep up my horsepower." I quickly realized I had done it again. I wasn't sure where all the horse talk was coming from.

He gave me a strange look. I leaned my head forward, returning his stare. My cheeks puffed up, I blew a solid breath, and I made a loud flapping sound with my lips to sound like a horse's neigh. Calvin laughed hysterically at the sound.

We stopped laughing when Singh walked in with six or seven of his guys. "Hey, there he is! The man of the hour, Mr. John."

Christ. I could barely sit for a few minutes in this town before everyone came looking for me. They were like dogs ready to pounce on you as soon as you walked through the door. Singh sat down at my table.

"You were right about that shipment last night. I intercepted Sonny and some of his guys. We caught him by surprise, for sure. We outnumbered them by about three to one. We killed several of them."

I sat there, continuing to look at him.

"Hey, just so you know, John. No hard feelings about what happened earlier with you and Adeepa. Oh, and those two guys I sent after you, it was just business. I hope you understand." He gave me a pat on the back.

"Sure, just business," I responded back.

"Hey, since you helped me out, I wanted to return the favor. I got my best guy, Lasal, working a job tomorrow. The prime minister has been a thorn in my side. He's got a mistress on the side, and I just wanted to send a little message. I'm sending Lasal to take her out. I got inside information from one of my informants within the administration that the two of them will be out on a boat cruise not too far from here. I got their full itinerary. He's taking her to a nice restaurant as a surprise. We have her assassinated, word gets out, and then it is all over the news. Eventually, it will ruin him, and he'll be out of my hair for good."

I just spotted my next opportunity. "How's the pay?"

Singh snorted. "It's a two-man job only, so you'll get fifty percent. Trust me, it's a nice cut. You haven't met Lasal yet, have you?"

I shook my head, but I had heard a lot about him.

"I'll tell you what. I'll come back over here tonight and introduce you two. We will discuss the plans in more detail. If you like what you hear, then I'll count you in. How's that sound?"

I nodded in approval. "Okay."

Singh and his men exited the restaurant. As soon as they walked out the door, Calvin rushed over.

"Shit, are you working for Singh now?" he asked in his usual excited tone.

"Will you relax? Oh, get me a scotch on the rocks. I wasn't gonna drink today, but now I need one."

He smiled and ran to get my drink. He came back less than a minute later.

"So, you said there are no working phones anywhere here?"

"Well, one of my coworkers has a mobile phone with roaming service from a foreign company. He actually gets a decent signal here."

"Really? What service is it?"

"Well, I'm not su—" Calvin started to reply.

"Never mind, What about the Kundali? They don't have working phones there, do they?" I asked.

"Oh, James definitely has working phones at his place. He has to because of all the people he deals with in Australia. He pays top dollar to keep the landlines in the hotel working. As for Singh, he doesn't require the phones since he knows everyone in a stone's throw from here to India," Calvin gushed gleefully as if he was proud of his knowledge.

"Can I borrow that phone from your coworker?"

Calvin stared at me with a curious look.

"Pretty please?" I said sarcastically.

"Who you going—"

"Don't ask. Can you help me or what? You're a nosy kid, you know that? But you're okay." I pointed at him, laughing.

"Okay, okay. Yes, I'll ask to borrow the phone." Calvin chuckled.

"Thank you."

CHAPTER 20

The phone at the Kundali hotel was on its fifteenth ring. You'd think the place was deserted. Finally, on its sixteenth ring, a voice answered.

"For fuck's sake! Why doesn't anyone answer this goddamn thing?" Sonny's voice erupted into the speaker. "Yeah, who is it?"

"Who's this? Sonny?" I spoke into the cell phone.

"Yeah. Who's this?"

"Oh, don't tell me you forgot about me already. I'm heartbroken. The nobody from out of town. I got a message for James."

"We don't need any messages from fucks like you. Our shipment got stolen last night. Three of our guys plus the three boatmen were murdered right in front of my eyes! You did this! It had to be you. You son of a bitch! I find it funny that he knew when and where it was gonna happen, especially since you were the only other one with the information."

"Don't be a moron. I may not work for you guys, but that doesn't mean I can't help you out. I'm gonna give you a chance to get even."

"Oh yeah? How?"

"I heard a rumor that Lasal is working a job tomorrow. He's going after some big shot politician. Well, his mistress, actually, but what do I know? Maybe it's all bullshit."

Silence on the line.

"You there?" I asked.

"Yeah, I hear you. All bullshit," he said in a sarcastic tone.

"Good. I'll tell you more details later. Now you tell James to watch his ass." I ended the call.

The Sri Lankans were definitely still in control, but anything could change in Mehliana.

• • •

I came downstairs from the apartment and walked back into the restaurant. I handed Calvin the phone.

"Tell your friend I said thanks."

"Sure thing."

The restaurant had emptied out. It was just me, Calvin, and two of the workers who were now cleaning up in the kitchen.

"I got a question. Do you think I could borrow a car? My tire is flat and being worked on next door. Also, I don't want anyone to see me leave later. It would be best if I could sneak out unnoticed. I know everyone is watching me closely."

"I got an old buddy of mine who gave me one of his spare vehicles a while back before he fled town. I don't use it much, and I haven't fired it up in a while, so I can't say how good it's going to run. It's parked several blocks away. I can give you the keys and the address. You're welcome to try it."

"That would be great."

Calvin ran upstairs and returned with the keys and the address a few minutes later.

"Thank you, my friend. Please, don't say a word to anyone."

"No worries. Not a soul," he said. "You can trust me, John."

"I know, Calvin, I know." I patted him on the shoulder.

CHAPTER 21

Several hours had passed, and it was almost five in the evening. I was sitting outside on the restaurant patio. In the distance, I saw Singh with a man I hadn't yet seen, but I knew who he was in an instant. The man stood about five-eight, was muscular but not gigantic, and weighed about one hundred and eighty pounds. A well-groomed beard and hair, green eyes, and a tanned complexion adorned his face. It would be easy for him to pass for Italian or Mediterranean descent. There's no telling where those mysterious green eyes came from. They were definitely his most remarkable feature. A bit creepy looking, to be honest. He was wearing a white tank top with dark jeans. He had various tattoos on his arms, and some on his face and neck. I couldn't make out all the letters and symbols displayed on his body, but I found all that ink quite distracting. I did notice a tiny teardrop under his left eye and a solid black star on the side of his neck.

"This is Lasal." Singh gave his usual sleazy car salesman smile.

Lasal said nothing. This guy was no doubt as cold-blooded as they come. I bet he was as bad as Adeepa, if not worse. Standing up, I climbed down the steps and down onto the dirt to get a better view of him. We stared at each other for what seemed like an eternity.

"This old man? He's the one who killed Adeepa?" Lasal said in a low, raspy voice. "I bet this geezer wets the bed at night."

"I bet I could still kick your ass," I said, glaring hard at him.

He gave me a hard shove, pushing me back several feet. I was ready to tango.

"Hey, enough!" Singh pulled out his gun and fired a shot into the air.

Lasal was caught off guard by the shot, momentarily forgetting about me.

"Enough. You guys can duke it out all you want afterward. I'm trying to arrange a business deal. Business comes first. You don't want to fuck this deal up, do you, Lasal?" Singh was obviously annoyed.

"How much we talking here?" I asked.

"Ah, that's the spirit." Singh smiled. "Fifty million Sri Lankan rupees is what I will pay. You each get half, so twenty-five million each. That rounds out to around a hundred twenty-five thousand U.S. dollars each, and you don't even have to do much, John. I mainly want you there as backup for Lasal in case any of the prime minister's security comes after you two."

"Why me?" I asked.

"I want to use the least amount of manpower as possible. If I'm there, I'll be tied to the murder. Lasal here is discreet. He is my best guy, but my next best guy you already killed, so I figured that makes you the next best guy. Get it?"

I nodded. "Okay, when and where?"

"All right, let's all take a walk somewhere, away from any prying ears," Singh said. The three of us strolled for several minutes, past the police station, past Singh's building, down a couple blocks, until we were alone. We hashed out all the details about what I would do specifically. After a good thirty minutes, we walked back in the other direction. As we walked by the police station again, I caught Kanish sitting on a wooden chair outside pretending to read a newspaper. His eyes were fixed on us. Singh nodded to Kanish, and Kanish returned a nod back. Lasal paid no attention to Kanish. I chuckled to myself again. I'm sure Kanish wanted to know what the three of us were planning. As we passed him, I felt his eyes burning a hole in my back.

We went our separate ways, Singh back to his building, and Lasal stepping into the building just next to it.

CHAPTER 22

A little past nine that night, I tiptoed out of the apartment, exiting through the back of the restaurant. I made sure no one was loitering nearby. I had the address Calvin had given me for the vehicle. I had studied a map earlier, so I was pretty sure where to go. I double-backed several streets just in case someone happened to be looking. I didn't want to take a chance with anyone—the fuel attendant, the inspectors, Singh, the restaurant workers, no one. The only person I had any trust in at all was Calvin. I figured he wouldn't double-cross me as long as I paid him well for the room and food service. Besides, I felt he looked up to me in a way. I could read it in his body language.

My walk lasted about fifteen minutes without a single soul in sight. I found the street, explored more, and finally spotted the building I was looking for. I saw a beat-up old shack and the vehicle parked under the carport Calvin had described. It was a blue Force Motors Trax that resembled a Jeep. It appeared to be a late-nineties model. The doors were unlocked. I got in, put the key in the ignition, and turned it to the right. The engine made a grinding noise. I gave it several seconds and turned it off.

"Well, shit. It figures." I let out a heavy sigh. "Okay, let's try this again."

I had to try it a few more times before it finally started up. I sat there, letting it warm up for a few minutes. This vehicle had obviously not been used in a while. I turned the headlights on and headed toward the Kundali, making sure not to drive anywhere someone could spot me. Once I was a reasonable distance away, I relaxed a bit.

• • •

When I finally arrived at the hotel, I parked in front. I walked in. As usual, several of James's crew were hanging out inside the lobby and kitchen area. Lana had come down the stairs after I had entered. She flipped her hair subtly with her hand, glanced at me, and stood off to the side.

"John." James came to greet me. "Did you tell Singh about our shipment? Sonny was scared shitless last night. They killed several of our guys." He had a rather serious look on his face.

"I heard about it, but I was out of town yesterday. I had to take some time for myself. I didn't say anything to Singh, but he did come to see me. He told me he knew you guys had jacked one of his shipments a while back and wanted to get even. I didn't know anything about what he was gonna do last night," I lied.

James stared into my eyes, trying to tell if I was telling the truth.

"I came to give you some more details about tomorrow," I said. "Singh thinks he hired me, but I wanted to help you out. I had to make it look convincing."

Sonny had walked into the lobby, followed by Jim, Randy, and two others.

"So, I met this Lasal guy, a real character, weird green eyes." I sneered, making circles over my eyes with my hands, mocking Lasal. "Singh wants to take out the prime minister's mistress. It's gonna happen at this restaurant near Colombo. I'm supposed to ride with Lasal. I'm just there to protect Lasal in case any of the security personnel try to get him."

Sonny interrupted, "I don't trust you."

James also appeared hesitant but seemed interested in what else I had to say. "So, what's your game plan?"

"Lasal and I will ride together out toward Colombo. I figured you could intercept us and take him out right there. I'll act just as surprised as he is, and we just take it from there."

"How do we know you won't try and double-cross us?" James asked.

"Yeah! This son of a bitch isn't on any side. He's playing both teams for his own agenda."

"You'll just have to trust me. You've said it yourself: I've dropped several of Singh's guys on my own. This valuable information could put you another step closer to running this town all by yourself. You know things would be much smoother without Singh's gang." I gave a sly grin.

"You have a good point. Stay for a drink?" James asked.

"No alcohol for me tonight, but if you got some leftover grub . . ."

"We do. Lana made curry today, a local dish. She is useful sometimes. Lana, you go to the kitchen and take care of him." He nodded at me. "I have some personal business matters to discuss with my men. If you'll excuse us, I'm sure you will be fine with Lana."

I nodded at James. Lana came over, and we walked to the kitchen together.

• • •

"So, you're back again." She smiled at me.

"Yup—I haven't run away, yet."

"Are you feeling okay?"

"I'm fine—why?"

"Do you mind me asking? How old are you?"

"I'm old enough. I'm a big boy. I pick up after myself. I even fold my own clothes." I smirked.

"Look. I-I just want to say . . ." She looked frightened.

"What's wrong? Are you in some sort of trouble, Lana?"

She gave a fake laugh while flipping her hair again off to the side. "Every one of us in this town is in some kind of trouble, John. This is not a good place to be. You and I both know that. You're different from these people. You're not what I initially thought."

I looked at her. She had gotten my sincere attention.

"The people here don't care about anything. They're cold, cruel, and greedy. They just come in looking to take advantage of someone or—" she stopped. "They just all act like they're better than everyone. Other people's lives mean nothing."

"Everyone is on some sort of high horse, only caring about themselves, you mean?"

She nodded. I could see tears in her eyes.

"James wasn't as evil before we came to this place. He always had shady dealings, but this town, it changes people. When I saw what you did the other day, it really scared me watching you with Sonny," she said.

"Oh, our little brawl? It's in man's nature to fight. Sorry if that little spectacle startled you."

"Not the fight. I'm talking about after, the way you changed. You . . . you don't remember, do you? You're not well, John."

"Of course I am. I'm perfectly fit." I slapped my stomach.

"No, up here." She pointed to her head.

I looked at her blankly.

"I wish I could get out of this place. Can you help me get out of here?" Lana leaned in close—whispering into my ear, "You're a good man. I could help you get the help you need."

I was still confused as to what she was talking about. I stared into her eyes.

Then, I heard James and his men approaching the kitchen. We quickly recomposed ourselves. Lana set a bowl in front of me, my third serving of curry today.

He entered. "Everything okay here?"

I gave a thumbs-up and quickly scarfed down the food. "Yeah, I've gotta get going."

"Be ready for tomorrow."

"Yeah," I said.

I walked outside, got in the car, put my madras hat on, and drove away.

The drive back was uneventful. Not much to tell. I couldn't help thinking about what kind of mess I had gotten myself into. I really didn't know what in the Christ I was doing anymore. Lana was scared. Could I help her? I didn't know. What did she mean when she said she was worried about me?

It was just after midnight when I parked the car back at the beat-up shack I had taken it from and headed back to the restaurant. I decided I would enter through the front door this time. No one would probably see me anyway. Just as I was about to ascend the front patio steps, I heard a voice from behind me.

"Where have you been out to tonight?"

I turned around to see Inspector Khan behind me, lighting a cigarette. Better Khan than Kanish because, with no witnesses, I probably would've dropped Kanish right here.

"Just out for a walk. I don't sleep much," I said.

"You drive anywhere tonight?" he asked.

"Well, I can't really do that 'cause my car is in the shop. It's got a flat. Unless someone's got a horse I can ride, I'm not goin' anywhere." I pointed inside the garage at the fuel station. My car was clearly visible from the shop window.

"I see. That's unfortunate," Khan said, continuing to puff on his cigarette.

"Shit happens."

"So, I got a question to ask you, John."

My ears perked up.

"There were a couple of women in Singh's group. Actually, they talked with you just before those two guys tried to shoot you. Mali and Tehani, I believe, are their names. Singh has been asking around about them. No one seems to have any information. Would you happen to know what happened to them? Did you kill them too? We didn't find their bodies, but I figured I'd ask."

"I wouldn't hurt them. You know that," I scoffed.

"Perhaps, though I'm not really sure what you would do. Sometimes it seems as if you care too much, and at other times it's like you have zero principles. You're an odd duck."

"Everybody in this town is odd if you ask me."

"Never a shortage of witty responses from you." He chuckled. "Good night, John." He walked off, then turned back to me. "You're treading real thin right now. I'd watch yourself 'cause if you're not careful, you will end up broke and dead."

I ignored him and went inside.

CHAPTER 23

The following day I got up later than expected. Every once in a blue moon, I slept late. It was after nine o'clock. As I stood in front of the mirror, I was confronted by my baggy eyes. I had quite the scruffy look going on. Definitely not the clean-cut image I had when I first arrived. I hadn't shaved in several days. I reached into my bag, pulled out my straight razor, and placed it on the sink counter. I splashed some warm water on my face, took out the Barbasol can, and sprayed some shaving cream into my hand. I patted my face and worked the razor. Several minutes later, I heard a car door slam outside. I looked outside my second-story window to see Sonny driving off. What the hell was he doing out here? I went back into the bathroom and quickly finished my shave. A moment later, I made my way downstairs. Calvin was in the kitchen making himself some breakfast. I peeked my head in.

"Thanks again for letting me borrow that car. It was much easier than taking a horse and buggy." I laughed inside my head, realizing I'd done it again.

Calvin gave me that look of confusion. He was about to say something before I cut him off. "Did anyone else come in here this morning?"

"No, I haven't seen any customers in here yet. Why?" he replied with a confused look.

"Be right back." I walked outside to the fuel station.

I saw my car had been moved from the garage and was parked outside. I saw the attendant, whose name I still didn't know, cleaning the windows.

"How's my car?"

"I repaired your tire. Good as new," he said.

"Will this cover the expenses?" I handed him a stack of rupees.

"Twenty thousand rupees? That's way more than needed. But I'll take it, and give you some extra information for it. A guy came around here asking me about this car. You just missed him by a few minutes."

"Oh yeah?" I said curiously.

"He asked if there was any registration or paperwork. He wanted to check your name."

"What did you say?"

"I didn't say anything, but he went into that car and dug around anyway. But guess what?"

"He didn't find what he was looking for, did he?"

"Nope."

"Well, you've earned that money. This guy, did he say what his name was?"

"He didn't say, but I know who it was. It was one of those Aussies. His name is Sonny."

I nodded. "Thanks."

Not a good sign. I opened the car and checked under the seat. The box of ammo was still there, untouched. Well, at least there's that. I grabbed it and headed back inside the restaurant and upstairs to the apartment.

• • •

I didn't want to take any chances. I reloaded my guns, and took a spare magazine and stuck it inside my pocket. In the midafternoon, Lasal and Singh came by. They asked me to walk with them down the block to their place. We entered Singh's building, and his men watched us enter a room together before Singh shut the door behind us.

"Just wanted to make sure we are all ready for this tonight," he said.

"As long as I'm getting paid, I'm ready." I gave a fake grin. The three of us sat down at a table.

Lasal was not amused in the slightest. I could tell he didn't want anything to do with me, but it wasn't his call. Singh threw a large stack of rupees onto the table that landed before me, forming a large pile.

"That's half. You'll get the rest after the job is done."

CHAPTER 24

Later that day, at around five o'clock, it was showtime. Lasal and I got into a midsized SUV. He was in the driver's seat—literally and figuratively. We drove for about an hour and a half, but it felt like it had been all day. We were about thirty minutes from where the job was to take place, a dirt road in the middle of nowhere, and it was the spot where I was expecting something to happen.

Four vehicles were suddenly behind us. Two of them sped ahead and stopped while the other two blocked us from behind.

"What the fuck is this!" Lasal looked at me suspiciously.

"No idea." I shrugged.

Sonny got out of one of the vehicles.

"Get out, Lasal, you fuck!" Sonny banged on the driver's-side window with his gun. "Oh, and you, too, you son of a bitch!" He gestured at me. Lasal and I looked at each other. The two of us exited the vehicle.

Sonny and nine other guys surrounded us. I made sure to remain at least a dozen steps away from Lasal 'cause I didn't want to get caught in the crossfire.

"Your boss stole our shipment and killed several of our guys at Dondras!" Sonny screamed while glaring angrily at Lasal. "Now it's time for us to get even."

"Get even? Your people have been meddling in our affairs for a while. Singh knows James stole one of our shipments a while back. You are not innocent. Fuck you."

"Well, you're done. Your life is over now. You can bet your ass on that." Sonny had the gun jammed against Lasal's forehead, pressing into his skin.

Lasal showed no fear. With lightning-quick reflexes, he snatched the gun from Sonny's hand and grabbed him by the throat, inserting the gun barrel into his mouth.

James's men aimed their guns at Lasal and shouted at him.

"Let him go!"

"Put him down now!"

"We will shoot you dead!"

Voices were screaming. I couldn't distinguish who was who.

"No way in hell I'm letting him go! You all will shoot me anyway! I may as well take this cocksucker down with me!" Lasal moved the barrel across Sonny's mouth. "Taste that metal, you little bitch." Again, poor Sonny, frightened to death, or soon to be, at any rate. He sure was terrible at portraying the tough guy.

Amid all this commotion, I stepped farther back. Several more vehicles pulled up. Surely James was going to appear soon. I realized I was wrong. Singh and all his men came out, probably around eighteen of them in all.

"John, you told these guys the plan, huh? I knew it. I knew you would double-cross me. You took us all for fools, playing both sides. I know a snake when I see one." Singh scowled at me.

"It takes one to know one," I retorted.

This set him into a frenzy. "I'm really fucking tired of you, foreigner! My ears are tired of your mouth, so I'll send you to the other side," he said as he aimed his gun at me with spit flying from his mouth.

At that moment, Sonny struggled furiously to shake Lasal off. A moment later, the two of them tumbled onto the ground, each struggling to grab the gun. Singh turned his attention to them.

I used the distraction to my advantage, backing farther away from the crowd and creating more space between them and me. Anything could happen now. Seeing Lasal regain control, I watched as he held Sonny by the back. He put the gun barrel against the back of Sonny's head.

"Say goodbye to this gutless coward!" Lasal pulled the trigger.

As soon as I heard the bang, I bolted away. I didn't want to lose any time. I heard tons of gunshots. I knew there was a chance someone would shoot me in the back as I ran, but my hope was that the two gangs would be too busy shooting at each other to notice me. I don't think I had run that hard in over fifty years. I heard people screaming at each other, someone shouting, "Sonny!" I'm pretty sure I heard Singh yelling several obscenities, but all the sounds blended together as I got farther away. I just kept running, like Forrest goddamn Gump, and I didn't look back.

CHAPTER 25

AUSSIES/SRI LANKANS

Sonny's brains had splattered everywhere. Lasal released him, letting his body fall lifelessly to the dirt with a loud thud. He immediately started shooting at James's men. He hit a couple of them before bullets penetrated his body.

"Shoot that motherfucker dead!" voices screamed. Lasal's body wiggled and shook as the bullets impaled him. His green eyes were open wide, and he gritted his teeth like a crazed madman—a dead one at that. His body finally dropped to the ground.

Singh and his men fired at James's shooters. Singh easily outmanned them, and they executed eight out of the nine men. They all dropped like flies. One last young kid remained. He pleaded for his life. Singh's men were about to shoot him dead before Singh yelled out at them. "No! Don't shoot him!" Singh walked up to him and grabbed him from the back of his head. "What's your name?"

The kid was breathing heavily. "R-Randy. P-please d-don't kill me," he stammered. "I'll do anything you ask."

"Today is your lucky day, kid. You are going to be the messenger boy. You got your pick of vehicles to choose from here. You get in and run your ass back to James and tell him what happened. Make sure he knows who runs things around here. You got that, boy?"

Randy nodded while his entire body quivered in fear.

"Well, what the hell are you waiting for? Hurry up before I change my mind." Singh and the rest of his men exploded in laughter. Singh fired a shot in the air. Randy screamed, which made Singh laugh louder. The kid bolted into one of the vehicles—he watched him speed away.

"What a chickenshit." Singh looked at his men, who all laughed in unison.

Singh looked at all the dead bodies—Lasal, Sonny, and the eight other men. He was upset that in a matter of days, he had lost both Adeepa and Lasal, but James had much less manpower now. Singh might be able to eliminate James once and for all. Suddenly, he remembered John.

"Where the fuck did that American bastard go?" he asked. "Anyone see which way he went?" Everyone shook their head. "He couldn't have gotten far. Search the area, spread out." Everyone got back in their vehicles to scour the terrain.

CHAPTER 26

I ran like my ass was on fire. I must have been running for at least five minutes or more. On our way, Lasal and I had seen nothing but dirt and rocks around us, but when I was running, I noticed trees in the distance. It was a small forest. I didn't have much time before someone would come after me. I guess Lasal was dead, and Singh and his guys were going to be hot on my trail. I got to the wooded area and ran through the trees, branches smacking me in the face. Eventually, after what felt like forever, I spotted a barn next to a small cottage. I banged on the door. An older man and his wife answered.

"I need to hide here. Men are after me." They didn't understand me at all. I reached into my pocket and gave them a large stack of bills. Their eyes got wide.

"Take it. Take it all. It's yours. Go. I don't want you to get hurt," I said.

The man started counting it and shaking his head. I pulled one of my guns. They both gasped, raising their hands high in the air.

"Run! Run! Get out of here!" I waved my hands at them. I pulled out some more bills, shoved them in the man's pocket, and shooed him away. They were both scared and confused, wondering why I was giving them money, but they gladly accepted it.

I pointed in the direction from where I had come. "Bad men are coming here! You go now!" I made the shooing motion again. They both nodded at me as if they understood, staring back at me as they ran off.

Christ. Now what the fuck would I do? What the fuck was I even doing? I had to think of something quick, or I'd be a dead man.

CHAPTER 27

JAMES

James heard the gunshots. He didn't trust John, and he anticipated he might try to double-cross him. The American wasn't on anyone's side and was clearly in it for himself. He had underestimated how much damage he was capable of. Earlier, James had waited just down the street from Singh's residence building and had shadowed them, purposely staying back a safe distance along with half his men.

He pulled over half a mile from where Sonny had intercepted Lasal and John. He pulled his binoculars out to get a better look. He saw several men drop, but was too far away to make out who they were, but he did see Singh's vehicles drive away.

Randy pulled up in another vehicle, practically jumping out of the car. "He killed them all! They're all dead! All of our guys!"

"Fuck. What about John? Is he dead too?"

"Not sure, I can't recall."

"C'mon, let's go take a look," James said.

They both drove out to where the bloodbath had occurred minutes earlier. Upon arriving, James examined all the men. Nine of the ten bodies were his. The only person Singh had lost was Lasal. Sonny was always a pain in the ass, but he had always been loyal to James. There would be hell to pay. He searched the area for John's body, but it was nowhere to be found.

"They couldn't have gotten far."

"The tire tracks go down that way." Bill pointed north.

"Okay, we're gonna end Singh once and for all. Let's go get this son of a bitch." James was pissed. "Keep an eye out for John too."

CHAPTER 28

I purposely left the front door of the house wide open. As I removed my shirt, I ripped it up a little bit. After a quick digging around the house, I found another spare shirt, a lightweight collared short-sleeve button-up. I threw my ripped shirt on the ground just outside the doorway as I stepped outside. Then I dashed out to the barn. I entered, scanning the room. The nearest place to hide was on the top of a large haystack in the corner. Nearly a story tall, I climbed to the top. Near my position was an open window. I could jump out for a quick escape if I needed to, though it was a drop of at least fifteen feet. My old self might actually break something if I didn't land properly. I stood on the haystack peering out the window. I could just barely see the front door of the house I had exited minutes earlier. Then I sat down again, out of the window's view, and I waited.

Maybe ten minutes later, I heard several vehicles pull up outside. Seconds later, doors slammed.

Now Singh was talking. "He must be here somewhere. Find him."

"We will get him, boss," another man's voice said.

I raised myself slightly and peered out the window, positioned on all fours. The entire crew was there. About twenty of them in all. It was gonna be tough to take them all out by myself if it came to it. The odds against me were so high that I had almost no chance of surviving another encounter. At this point, keeping myself hidden was the best option.

"Hey, boss! I found his shirt. The door was open. He must be inside," a man said.

Good—they'd taken the bait. That would buy me time.

"Let's go. I want four or five of you to stay out here, though, and keep a lookout," said Singh.

Footsteps could be heard as they entered the house. I did not have to wait long before they realized I wasn't there. Next, they would check the barn. I would be spotted if I ran out right now. I guess I could take my chances and try to shoot them all.

A moment later, more vehicles pulled up. Gunshots rang out within seconds, and I heard men screaming in agony. Car doors flew open and slammed shut. I inched closer to the window and peered outside. James and several of his men were standing outside the house with firearms in hand. Five lifeless bodies were lying on the ground before James.

"It's over! You're dead! You hear me, Singh?" James shouted toward the house. "All right, fellas, let's finish this!"

I frantically ducked back down, trying to figure out precisely what to do next. Multiple shots were fired from both parties. It was hard to see everything going on, but I saw James light a Molotov cocktail and throw it into the house, causing a loud crash. Seconds later, I heard another window break and looked out again to see that the house was on fire. I was glad I had been able to run the homeowners away in the nick of time. James was gonna smoke everybody out. All of Singh's men who had stayed outside were now on the ground, dead. Shots fired out at James from inside the house. Now was the perfect time to jump out the window.

I fell to the ground with a thud—without hurting myself. I looked around. The barn was far enough away from the house, and the shooting was loud enough so that I remained unnoticed. I ran in the opposite direction, and then I double-backed to the location of James's vehicles. They had parked a bit farther from the house than Singh. I picked a random car and slid underneath it, making myself perfectly still, trying to control my breathing. *Oh, John, this is probably a really stupid fucking idea*, I thought to myself, but I also knew it was the best I could think of on such short notice.

CHAPTER 29

JAMES/AUSSIES

James and his men had slain most of Singh's. Those who were left couldn't be many. They threw enough Molotov cocktails inside the house to kill everyone who remained. If they smoked them out, they would be easy to shoot down. He just hoped John would show up sooner or later. Singh must be executed as quickly as possible. Nevertheless, he had a different plan for John if he came out. Although he preferred not to kill him right away, if he was to die in the fire, so be it.

As more of the house started to go up in smoke, James and his men continued waiting. A man threw himself out the second-story window, crashing through the glass and onto the dirt ground. He got up, his body on fire, and James's men mowed him down with a spray of bullets. More men bolted from the front; James and his entourage unloaded immediately. Four more guys fell to the ground. Screams of anguish erupted from inside as several men burned to death. Finally, Singh came out, hands raised. He got down on his knees and held his hands together in prayer.

"Please, have mercy! Let's make a deal," he begged.

"No." James laughed in his face. "This is my territory now." James held his pistol and fired multiple shots directly at Singh's chest. Singh's body shook every time it was hit, and he fell on his back, his eyes staring wide open at the sky above him.

James and his men stepped farther away from the house and waited fifteen minutes to see if any more of Singh's gang would come tumbling out. The house was eventually reduced to ashes as it burned to the ground. Several men coughed as smoke filled their lungs.

"Let's go. Everyone's dead. No way anyone that was in there is still breathing. Go check the barn and see if anyone is in there."

Several guys walked the barn perimeter and then searched inside.

"No one here, boss," Randy said.

"Okay, let's regroup back at the Kundali." James gave a hand signal, and everyone ran back to their vehicles and got in.

CHAPTER 30

I saw legs and feet running in my direction. I grabbed the vehicle's underside with my arms and did my best to secure my feet against a surface. Christ—this was gonna be rough.

The vehicle moved away quickly, but I managed to hang on well and tight. I couldn't see too well, but I concentrated on keeping a firm hold. There was absolutely no way in hell I was gonna hang on here for the entire ninety-minute ride back to town. I'd wait until the vehicle slowed, then I would drop off. There was still a good chance I'd get run over if there was a car behind me, but perhaps I could roll out of the way if we weren't moving too fast. Even if I managed to roll away safely, I could still get shot on the spot if James or any of his men saw me. I didn't have any other option, unfortunately.

Roads in this area were mostly dirt. We had not even entered the city of Colombo and were still out in the boondocks. This was good—as we weren't getting up to too high a speed. I guessed I had been hanging on for nearly twenty minutes when I finally decided to risk it and make my escape.

I dropped from the car and quickly rolled several times to the side. I moved and rolled at least six or seven times. If it was going to happen, this is where I was going to get shot. My body hit something. I felt my face get scratched, and I was dizzy. My head ached. I stared up at the sky. I heard the vehicles continue to keep moving. Nobody had stopped. Objects were digging into my back, but I was too tired to move. I waited for the dizziness to fade.

"Dad, you could've killed yourself. What were you thinking?"

"It's fine, Mallory. Everything is fine. I'm okay," I answered.

"Go back home. You need to get away from this horrible place."

"No, I gotta get back to finish this, once and for all. I have to see this through." I raised myself up off the ground. It had gotten darker, and I stared up at the evening sky. Looking down, I saw I had rolled right smack into several bushes. There were lots of them around here, and trees also. I touched my face and felt the blood from my scratches. I had scrapes on my arms. The shirt I had borrowed was ripped to shreds, the sleeves were missing, and it now resembled a shredded tank top of sorts. My guns and holster were much more noticeable without a proper shirt on. I had nothing else on me except some money, and was still an hour away from Mehliana by car. It was gonna be a long walk. Christ.

• • •

I had removed my holster, shoving a gun in each of my pants pockets. I folded the holster as best as I could, carrying it in my hand. After walking for an hour, I was exhausted. The damn cell phone still had no signal. I stared at the clock on my phone but couldn't read it. In fact, my vision was blurry due to the dirt being kicked up into my eyes during the drive. I was dehydrated and in desperate need of water. Hearing a car approaching from behind, I turned back and saw headlights.

Standing in the middle of the road, I waved my arms at a small pickup truck, which slowed for me. The driver was a Sri Lankan man, and in the passenger seat was a woman with a baby in her arms. I flashed them some rupees. I spoke English to them, but they greeted me in Sinhala instead. There was no sign that either of them knew English.

"Mehliana, yes? Mehliana." I pointed at myself. "I need to go Mehliana." I pointed at the truck bed in the back.

"Galle," the man said, pointing at himself and the woman. "Galle, okay?"

Galle was close enough, as I had stayed there before and knew the area well. I handed him the stack of rupees and quickly jumped in the back of the truck. I banged on the back of the glass from the truck bed until the window slid open.

"Water? Do you have any water?" I made a drinking gesture with my hand. The woman handed me a bottle of water. "Thank you." I gulped the bottle until it was empty and lay down in the truck bed.

It was a quiet ride of around forty minutes or so. We stopped outside the couple's home. I knew exactly where I was. Galle Beach was a short walk away. As I exited, I thanked them and went on my way. The pair waved and smiled at me, and I walked to a nearby hotel and checked in. I took a shower and got myself cleaned up. I would rest here for the night to get my bearings, and then head into Mehliana tomorrow to see Calvin.

I turned on the television. I hadn't watched television since I had last been here in Galle. I hadn't even spotted one in Mehliana anywhere, not that I had any time to watch anything. A documentary was on. The news anchorwoman spoke in English.

". . . Chinese Admiral Zheng was born into a Muslim family in 1371. From 1405 to 1433, Zheng completed many treasure-hunting missions. Sometime between 1410 and 1411, Zheng launched an attack on the island of Ceylon, the former name of Sri Lanka. An impressive nautical battle occurred between Chinese and local forces. The ship held massive treasures packed with gold, precious gems, silver, silk, and religious artifacts. Many were given as gifts to foreign leaders in exchange for other valuable items. The ship sank to the bottom of the Indian Ocean along with the fortune."

I sipped on a bottle of water while I continued watching.

"Now, more than six hundred years later, the items have still never been found. Although many history books have recorded the events, no one knows the exact number of ships that sank. There have been numerous archaeological expeditions and scuba dive searches to recover these lost treasures, but nothing has been found.

"Scientists and archaeologists have reportedly used advanced military equipment to conduct searches along the Sri Lankan coastline. Project details are kept secret, but there have been rumors that some of the shipwreck sites have been discovered."

That was enough for me. I flipped the TV switch off. I was tired and in desperate need of some shut-eye.

CHAPTER 31

The following day I slept late, until just past ten o'clock. I took another long shower and headed down to the lobby. There was a breakfast buffet with a mix of Western and local food. I ate a whole lot, drank a few cups of black coffee, and guzzled several bottles of water. Even though I had cleaned up the best I could, my clothing was still rather dirty. I'd have to wait to change until I got back to the restaurant since all my spare things were in my room.

I walked outside and looked for some taxis. I'd have to take my chances with the prices. The drive back was just under an hour. I saw several taxis out in front of the hotel. Some looked legit, and others not so much. I walked over to the first guy I saw.

"How much for a ride back to Mehliana?" I asked.

He stared at the ripped remnants of my shirt. "I don't go to that town, but I can get you real close to it. To Matara for fifteen thousand rupees, sir," the man responded.

Although it sounded like a rip-off, I had that much in my pocket plus a lot more. I just wanted to get back as quickly as possible. I fished out a stack of funny money, counting it and handing him exact change. His eyes lit up.

This was probably enough to last him a couple of weeks. He gestured for me to get in the back seat, and I hopped in. Hopefully, it would be a nice, quiet ride.

• • •

We had been driving for about thirty minutes. The driver was chatty. He told me his name, but I forgot it. I wasn't in the mood for small talk, but I did my best to pretend. I was curious to see if the town was still in one piece. He had been playing some sort of Sri Lankan folk music. Every few minutes, he would stare at me in the rearview and ask, "Is this good music? You like? You want to listen to something else?"

"Yeah, it's fine. I don't care. Whatever you want to listen to is fine."

The ride was bumpy. He changed the music again.

"You like The Beatles?"

"Uh-huh."

It felt like forever and a day, probably 'cause I was so tired, but we finally arrived at Matara. I thanked the driver, and he drove off, kicking up dirt everywhere as he did. I ended up walking a way to get back to Mehliana, but it was good exercise, I guess. Finally, I reached the restaurant. I looked outside and didn't see anyone except the fuel attendant. I stared back at the police station. I didn't see those gutless inspectors, but I'm sure they were looking at me from inside. I walked up the steps into the restaurant.

I entered. No other patrons. Calvin and two other restaurant workers were there. They all stared at me like a deer in the headlights when I walked in.

"Holy shit!" Calvin ran over to me.

"Holy shit, what?"

"We assumed you were dead."

"Not yet."

"James came around with a few of his guys. He told the inspectors that Singh and all his guys were dead. Said there was a big shoot-out between them. He mentioned there was a big house fire and that everyone was dead, including you."

"As you can see, I'm still standing. As Sir Elton John says." I grinned.

Calvin gave me another perplexed look. "Who?"

"One of these days, I need to give you a school lesson on pop culture. Never mind, I'm going upstairs. As you can see, I need to put on some clean clothes." I pointed at my shirt. "Did James say he was gonna come back here anytime soon?"

"I didn't hear anything."

I nodded and went to my apartment. I stripped all my dirty clothes off, put them into a plastic bag to toss later, and showered again. When I stepped out of the shower, I put on some clean clothing, including a regular shirt with sleeves intact.

Despite everything that had happened, I felt good. I had fucked up both the James and Singh gangs even though my kill count was only three total. I'm sure James was happy his squad won out in the end, and maybe he'd even forget about me. Maleesha had been avenged, with her tormentors all dead. I'd try to talk to her before I left town like I said I would. I'd probably head out tomorrow or the day after, and get the hell out of this shit town. It wasn't so much that the town was shit; it was more the people.

• • •

I came downstairs with my clean clothes on, feeling like a million bucks, or maybe more like a thousand bucks—a million was too generous after what I had been through. I sat down at a table in the far corner. It was around three o'clock in the afternoon.

"Okay, I've had my share of local curry. I'm going back to my comfort food. Give me a steak—medium-rare. Scotch on the rocks, too, please. I'll buy a round for you, Calvin, and everyone else who wants one," I barked at the other two workers.

They politely declined, explaining that they didn't drink. Funny enough, I still didn't know their names.

"C'mon, Calvin, have a drink." I gestured for him to sit down.

"Oh, maybe just one. I don't have much tolerance for alcohol."

"Bring the whole bottle and ice bucket. Extra glasses too." Calvin grabbed the items and returned, setting everything down on the table, one by one.

I snatched the bottle of scotch from him. He sat down. I poured into one of the Glencairn glasses till it was one-third filled. I scooped two block-shaped cubes from the ice bucket, plopping them into the Glencairn glass, which I then held in front of Calvin's face. He was excited like he never had anybody to hang out with, ever.

We clinked glasses.

"Cheers, buddy." I took a long mouthful and downed it.

"Cheers."

Calvin tried to do the same but ended up choking after he got half of it down.

"Steady, big fella." I firmly patted his back.

He coughed several times. "It burned my throat."

"Careful now. You'll make your throat hoarse."

He laughed. "Again with the horse?"

"Huh? No, not 'horse.' I said 'hoarse.'"

"It's the same word," he said.

"No—what I meant was h-o-a-r-s-e. With an *a*."

Calvin coughed again, almost choking to death. I patted him on the back. "You get used to it after a while." I waved to the other staff members to bring two more water bottles to the table, handing one to Calvin. He took a big gulp to ease his throat.

• • •

A couple hours later, I was pretty drunk. Calvin ended up having a few, but I probably had drunk twice what he had. I knew, at this point, I had to cut myself off. I had the workers bring us some large water glasses. They didn't seem to mind that Calvin had been sitting with me rather than working. Not one patron had come in that day.

I downed another large gulp of water and finished the bottle, probably my fourth or fifth one.

"So, did everybody in this town hightail it out of here or what?"

"I think folks are even more worried. People are dropping like flies, and nobody wants to be caught in the crossfire. How long are you planning to stick around, anyway?"

"The truth is, I'm probably gonna get the hell out of here by the day after tomorrow. I'm done with this town. No offense, you're great, but everyone else not so much."

"No, I get it. It is how it is, but you're a hero! Legend!" He clinked my glass.

"Yeah, well, I wouldn't say that, but I won't argue with you." I chuckled. "So, Calvin, how old are you anyway?"

"Twenty-three."

"No girlfriend, family?"

"No, I mean, I'd like to start a family, but I've been trying to save up to get out of this town. One of these days, I'm going to leave, but I can't right now. Just don't have the finances."

I nodded.

"What about you, John? You don't talk much about your personal life. Everyone in this town has been wondering about you since you got here. Do you have a family?"

I stared at him, and then I looked off to the left, thinking back about my family. "They're all gone now. All gone," I whispered.

"You mean they're not alive anymore?"

I shrugged. "It doesn't matter anymore." One of the workers brought another bottle of water, setting it down in front of me, and I drank it.

"How many more glasses of scotch you gonna have?"

I sighed. "I'm done." I stood up. "Can I get two more bottles of water, please?" I looked over at the workers.

One of them fetched the water bottles for me.

"I'm gonna retire early tonight. I'm a bit tired now, and I need to detox," I said, holding the two bottles of water in front of me.

"Okay, John, you sleep well. Thank you for the drinks. It was a pleasure hanging out and getting to know you better, sir. I wish you could stay in Sri Lanka."

I nodded, patted him on the shoulder, threw down a bunch of rupees in front of Calvin, and headed upstairs.

•••

I sat at the edge of the bed, waiting for the alcohol to wear off. I definitely had one too many. I've been worse, though. By tomorrow morning, I'd be fine. I'd probably finished ten bottles of water by now and be pissing the rest of the night away, but the water was good to help get rid of the buzz. It was also hot as hell outside. The wind picked up so much dirt that you could practically taste it. I regretted drinking all that scotch. It was careless on my part. I looked around the room, gulped down another bottle of water, and took my shirt off. I fell back onto the bed, letting out a deep exhale.

Somehow, I had the feeling I was skating on thin ice. Inspector Khan's voice came into my head. He had given me a little warning when I had seen him in the middle of the night a couple of days ago. It's funny how life works out. For a minute, you think you're going to get away with it all scot-free. But you end up paying the price. No exceptions. Everybody pays the price, even a nobody like me who has nothing. I drifted off to sleep.

CHAPTER 32

I awoke just after two o'clock in the morning to the sound of my door being kicked in. I tried to reach for my guns, but I was grabbed by several hands and thrown off the bed. The lights came on. All I could see were feet and fists coming down on me. A boot hit my stomach and knocked the wind out of me. I was turned onto my back, and I stared up at James and eight other men.

"He's nothin' without his guns," one of the men said. Bill, I think it was.

Randy punched me right in the mouth. I tasted the blood on my teeth and around my lips. I was still a bit hungover. I laughed.

"You hit like a girl," I said to him.

"Motherfucker!" He brought his fist back again, but James held him back.

James hovered over me. "I know it was you, John. I know you told Singh about my drug shipment at the pier. I'm sure you also told him that you told us about the job with Lasal. You've been playing both sides this whole time. You lured us all out there, hoping we'd all get killed. Isn't that right?"

I looked up at James. "I didn't tell Singh that I informed you about the job with Lasal. I didn't like him any more than you did."

"Well, you're not on our side either. You double-crossing liar."

"Fuck you, James. You're a clown, and so is your joker gang here—a bunch of half-wits."

He squatted over me and punched me in the face. "Fuck me? Fuck me? You asked for it." He pummeled me with lefts and rights, his men holding me down, and all I could do was take it. I was picked up, dragged down the stairs, and shoved into the back of a trunk.

CHAPTER 33

CALVIN

Calvin had heard the door open downstairs in the middle of the night. Shortly after, loud footsteps were running up the stairs. John's room was closest to the stairs, and he heard James and his men scuffling with John. Calvin quickly scurried out his door and into John's room, which was now empty. Evidence of the scrap was visible: the lamp had fallen from the nightstand near the bed, blood drops covered the floor, and dirt traces were scattered everywhere. His eyes scanned the room and found what he was looking for on the table: John's car keys. He snatched them up and quickly fled the room.

When he reached the top of the stairs, he saw John being dragged outside. Calvin ran down to the ground floor and stared out from inside the main door. He saw several men take turns punching John in the face before putting him in the trunk of one of the vehicles. When the vehicles pulled away, he ran next door to the fuel station to where John's car was parked. He got in, started the engine, and waited a moment before he drove off to follow them. He kept his lights off and stayed far behind. He could barely see them up ahead, but he already anticipated where they were headed.

He tailed James and his men almost to the Kundali hotel. He stopped just down the road and parked out of sight. He could see the hotel from a distance, but he was confident he wouldn't be noticed as long as he was quiet. He got out of his car and kept a lookout. He didn't have a plan, but he would hang around to keep watch. He wanted to help John, but he was scared. Unlike John, he was no hero. He wasn't sure what to do, but he didn't want to let down his only friend. No one else had ever given a shit about him. He got out of his car and walked toward the hotel. After walking several minutes, getting closer to the hotel, he suddenly noticed a pungent stench. And flies buzzing.

"What is that?"

He looked around and saw a large lump in the dirt. He pinched his nose and realized it was a human body. It looked like it had been here for several days. Unable to stand the stench, he almost threw up on the ground, but he managed to control himself and jogged away from it.

He panicked, ran back to the car, and stood there for another thirty minutes just watching. Nobody had stepped outside. He decided to take another look, running past the body so he wouldn't feel sick again. He approached the front steps, ascending as quiet as a mouse. He stared through the doorway glass, trying to see if he could spot anyone. There was no one in the lobby. He darted around hathe back side of the hotel, searching windows for light. At the rear of the hotel, he stared down at a basement window that had a faint light emitting from it. He got down on the ground. He saw John seated in a chair, a man holding his hands from behind. Calvin tried to listen to what they were saying.

"What? What d-do you want?" he heard John speak, barely conscious.

"To see you pay, that's what we want. Right, boys?" James stood tall in front of him. They poured a bucket of ice-cold water onto him. He gasped.

There was nothing Calvin could do, so he went back to his car and waited. He would stay all night if he had to. Maybe he could wait for the men to leave and somehow get John out. Calvin felt helpless and sad for his friend, but he wouldn't leave.

CHAPTER 34

I was in a basement room in the Kundali, sitting in a chair while a man held me down from behind, and men took turns punching me in the face and stomach.

"Admit it, John. You're scared," James said.

"He's nothin' without his guns," Bill cackled. The rest of the men exploded in laughter.

I had heard that same line back in my bedroom. "How many times you gonna repeat yourself, Bill?" Bill gave me a dirty look and gestured to Randy. Randy dumped a bucket of ice-cold water over my head. I gasped, accidentally swallowing some of it.

"Admit it! You're pissing in your pants right now, aren't you?" Randy snorted.

"The only thing I'm scared of is freezing to death from this ice water," I replied.

Randy gave me another one of his bitch slaps across the face. "You know you're scared. Admit it."

I wouldn't give him the satisfaction. "The water's gettin' cold." I smiled, tasting the blood on my lips.

I got hit with several more punches to the face. A left, then a right, then another left, and then I don't know what. Suddenly, everything fell out of focus, and I felt the room spinning. I saw a black pool surrounding me and then complete darkness.

CHAPTER 35

Brooklyn, New York, 1947

I'm seven years old, and I've just started third grade at Saint Esther Catholic School. My parents had decided to yank me out of my former school at South Brooklyn Primary—mainly my mother's choice. I was sad because I had friends there, unlike here where I knew no one. It was a sudden decision made just last month. My parents said Billy and I should be brought up in a proper Christian environment. My brother, Billy, was five years older than me and as many grades ahead. He had enjoyed his time at South Brooklyn Junior High last year and was equally disappointed about being transferred. In the integrated Junior–Senior High school, he was in eighth grade at Saint Mary's Catholic School across the street, which housed the seventh- to twelfth-grade students. He was older and tougher than I was, so I doubt he'd have much to worry about.

We were only three weeks into the school year, but it felt so much longer. It was much stricter here. The mood was grimmer, the halls less lit than South Brooklyn, and the temperature noticeably colder. I was constantly freezing. It was also strange being only around other boys instead of the usual co-ed setting. We all had uniforms, and everyone looked exactly the same with the same black slacks, white shirts, school-colored ties, and either a black jacket or sweater. How dull.

I was sitting in my usual spot on the right side of the classroom—the third desk from the front. There were still a few minutes left before the tardy bell would ring. I flipped through my notes, trying to prepare for class. Suddenly, I felt a wad of paper hit the back of my head. I turned around and looked back to my left to see Andrew Clausen smirking in the back center row. A few of the boys sitting close to him were also giggling. I stared at them, keeping my gaze in their direction.

"What? What are you looking at, new kid?"

"Stop throwing stuff at me," I said.

"What are you gonna do about it? You say the same thing every day. 'Stop,' 'stop,' 'wah,' 'stop.'" The other boys laughed again. Several other boys in the classroom stared, merely observing. Andrew was a typical class bully, but he was also a popular kid. He knew everyone and came from a well-off family. His parents had connections and had donated thousands of dollars to the school each year. I turned back around, deciding to ignore them.

The first couple of weeks had started off okay. I tried to keep my head down and blend in with the rest of the kids. However, this last week had been hell. Andrew decided to target me since I was the new kid and all. Every day there were random moments where he would throw stuff or say stupid things, trying to get a rise out of me. I did my best to not take the bait, but it was hard. I knew I didn't want to get into any trouble, but being a pacifist takes its toll after a while. I had to be careful. He had already gotten me into some trouble on two separate occasions, including once in this same class. Several days ago, he had pulled the same stunt, and I confronted him. Sister Agatha hadn't witnessed Andrew in the act, insisting I was talking nonsense.

Also, in math class earlier this week, he had slapped me on the side of the head after walking by to sharpen his pencil. I stood up, but Sister Agnes had asserted I was the troublemaker. Andrew got away with a lot. He was good at making sure nobody was looking when he targeted someone. Father Jacob, the principal, thought highly of Andrew and his parents. I knew this because I had heard Andrew constantly brag to his friends about it. In the end, I didn't care if I got a slap on the wrist from the nuns. I could deal with it. I wouldn't tolerate a slap to the head from another boy, though.

The bell rang. A moment later, Sister Agatha walked into the classroom with her usual stern look. She was early- to midthirties, medium height, about five-seven, and an average build. This was the first class of the day: Social Studies.

"Okay, class. Turn to page two forty-six. Today we will be reviewing what you read for homework. Who can tell me when the American Revolution started?" She stared down at her notepad and flipped through some pages. There was a moment of silence.

"Anyone?" she asked as she continued flipping through pages without looking up.

Suddenly, I felt a large wad of paper nail me right in the back of the head. I looked behind me, before I quickly turned back around. A boy in the front row—Ricky Santorelli—raised his hand. Ricky was the teacher's pet. He answered every question when given a chance. Sister Agatha finally looked up, gazing at Ricky.

"Yes, Ricky?" Sister Agatha gave an inquiring expression.

"1765," he said.

"Yes, correct." Sister Agatha nodded in approval, turning around and approaching the blackboard. She grabbed a piece of chalk and started writing on the board.

I caught a glimpse of Andrew and his pals mocking Ricky. They had teased him for years, but Ricky kept his head down, and the kids now mostly left him alone, minus the occasional verbal ridicule.

A moment later, I felt the sharp end of a pencil hit me in the back of the neck. I turned around again to see Andrew laughing. I'd been dealing with this for the last week straight. I picked up the pencil and threw it right back at him. I had just missed his head. Sister Agatha turned around at the exact moment I threw it.

"Johnny Sandes!"

"He's the one who started it. He always does. You never see him in the act. I'm tired of this!" I stood up and pointed directly at Andrew.

Andrew looked at me and threw his hands up. "You're crazy. I didn't do anything, Sister. He's lying."

"Johnny, this is your third outburst this week. This is not a good start for you at Saint Esther. You have already been warned twice. You are coming with

me now to the principal's office. We will see what Father Jacob has to say about your rebellious ways."

I saw Andrew and his pals all displaying nasty grins. The rest of the students had worried expressions on their faces. I could hear various whispers arising throughout the room. Sister Agatha turned and shushed the whisperers in the room before leading me out the door into the hallway. She grabbed me firmly by the upper arm.

"Ow. That hurts," I yelped.

"Hush. Do as you are told, child." Her tone was harsh.

We descended down a stairwell to the lower floor. There were no classrooms on this level. This is where all the offices were, including Father Jacob's. She took me into an office area where several other nuns were sitting. I recognized a few of them—Sister Agnes, Sister Janice, Sister Carrie, and several others whose names I did not know.

"This student has caused another disruption today," Sister Agatha said.

They all stared at me with unsympathetic looks.

"Johnny Sandes. He's new here," one of the nuns said.

"Yes, we should take him to Father Jacob."

"No—probably best to not bother him. He will be irate, I'm sure. He has a lot on his plate right now," Sister Janice suggested.

"Well, we should tell him. He's been causing a lot of trouble for someone so freshly enrolled here. Several outbursts in the past week. Sister Agnes, didn't you say he did something similar recently in your class?"

"That's right. He was arguing with Andrew Clausen, an exemplary student."

"That's not fair. Andrew's always starting stuff with me. He's the trouble-maker," I blurted, having had enough of these false accusations.

"You will be punished now!" Sister Agatha screamed as she and the rest of the nuns escorted me down the hallway into another office room. This room was more spacious, with less clutter. I was shoved into the room.

Sister Agatha pulled me up to a desk, making me stand in front of it. She gestured to the other nuns, and they grabbed each arm, forcing my hands onto the table. They held my arms from the wrist so I couldn't take them off the table. Sister Agatha pulled out a ruler from a desk drawer.

She whacked my hand hard with a ruler. I felt a sharp pain on the tops of my knuckles. I jerked back, but the two nuns held my arms in place. I felt another hard whack on my other hand. This time I broke free, but two more nuns pressed their hands onto my back from behind. I felt two hands gripping each shoulder and another set of hands pressed against my lower back. More nuns were observing from inside the room. So many eyes were on me.

"This will teach you to misbehave, Johnny Sandes." She came down with several more strikes, rapping my right knuckles.

I started crying, unable to hold back any longer.

"Let me go!" I wailed.

They continued holding me in place, and I was unable to escape. Soon, another nun, whom I didn't recognize, came to my left side, carrying another ruler. They whacked each of my hands simultaneously. I shrieked and screamed several more times. I jerked and struggled, trying my hardest to break free.

The raps on my knuckles continued for what felt like an eternity. Eventually, the pain from the impact ceased, turning to numbness. My eyes stung from tears I was unable to wipe away. I could barely see anything, and my nose was running.

I stared down at my hands, covered with bloody cuts; several fingers were swollen. The whacking soon stopped, and my hands were released.

"Now, perhaps you have learned your lesson, Johnny. Now it's time to go back to class. We need to have you wash your hands first."

What? Back to class? Right now? No way. There was no way in hell I was going to go back in there. They led me back out into the hallway. I was fatigued. They beat the energy out of me. They escorted me down the hallway to just outside a public bathroom.

Sister Agatha gave me an uncaring look. "Go inside and wash your hands. Come back out as soon as you finish. We will wait for—" I bolted down the hallway with what little energy I had left.

I was already at the stairwell when I heard her yell, "Stop him!" I darted up the stairs and got to the main floor. By now, I heard several of the nuns screaming, "Stop that boy! Someone stop him!"

It was a long run down the hallway to the main exit. I ran, huffing and puffing. I blew by several classrooms and caught sight of people staring as I whizzed by.

"Somebody stop that boy!" Sister Agatha yelled again as she got to the main floor. I turned my head and saw more nuns, along with some schoolboys popping their heads out of the classroom. I turned my head back to the front as I continued running. I was about halfway to the main exit. Suddenly, a tall, heavyset nun emerged from the opposite end of the hall. She saw the commotion and slowly walked toward me.

Oh no! How was I gonna get past her? I continued running toward her. She was in front of a classroom that was closest to the exit. As I ran toward her, I faked left. She fell for it, reaching for me, but I quickly changed to go right. The heavy nun stumbled to the ground. I was now in the clear. I slammed up against the door, pressing it open, and barrel-assed outside and down the stone steps.

I could see boys yelling out at me from some of the classroom windows. I couldn't make out what everyone was saying. I thought I heard one kid yell, "Run! Run!" I ran out onto the pavement, but I had to make it outside the gate and off the school property before I was in the clear. The nuns were still chasing me! I went through the parking lot, heading toward the security gate. From a distance, I could see the guard still sitting in his booth staring down at something, probably a newspaper or book. He hadn't yet been alerted to what was happening. I continued to watch him as I ran, waiting for him to look up.

As I got closer, so did the nuns' screams. "Mr. Carson! Mr. Carson! Stop that boy! Stop him!"

Mr. Carson, the security guard, finally looked up and saw what was happening. He came out of his booth and ran toward me. With him in front of me, and the nuns on my tail, I was running out of options. I went left, running through more parked vehicles and toward the football field. A chain fence about eight feet high separated the field from the parking lot. The field also had an entrance gate, but it was too far away from me—on the other side of the lot. I would have to climb the fence. I jumped as high as I could onto the fence but only got about halfway up. I rose as fast as I could, falling over the top onto the soft grass on the other side. My body went down hard and knocked the wind out of me. The potent smell of grass filled my lungs. I looked up toward the goalpost, slightly ahead of me to the left.

The nuns and Mr. Carson were weaving through the parked cars—they had almost reached the other side of the fence from where I had just come. Mr.

Carson got to the fence first and started climbing. The nuns were now running down to the far side of the parking lot to the field's entry door. I quickly got up and started running to the other side of the field.

There was an even larger fence than the one I had just climbed to my right. It separated the field from the public street but was way too high for me to climb. First, I had to get across the field. If I could make it to the other side, past the opposite goalpost and bleachers, I could reach the exit door to that street. I was about one-third along the length of the field when I heard the thud of Mr. Carson falling from the fence and landing onto the grass. He actually climbed over it! I turned back and saw that he had also stumbled as I had, cursing to himself. As I continued to run, I looked to my back left and could see the nuns finally coming through the entry door. A couple of them had given up the chase and decided to stay back in the parking lot. They were gasping. Sister Agnes, Agatha, and a couple of the more youthful nuns kept up the chase.

I, now halfway across the field, was sweating profusely. The adrenaline coursing through my body masked the pain and throbbing in my knuckles.

"You will be sorry, Johnny Sandes!" I heard Sister Agatha shout.

Another minute later, I finally reached the other side, running past the goalpost and bleachers. Mr. Carson was the closest behind me, but I was still a reasonable distance ahead of him. I reached the exit opening and went through, running onto the street. Mr. Carson and Sister Agatha continued after me down the road. I ran to the next block, turned the corner, and stopped for a breath, thinking that I had lost them. I placed my hands on my knees and peered back around the corner. Sister Agatha and Mr. Carson saw my head pop out and came after me again.

I was out of options. I started running again. Up ahead, I spotted the streetcar, which was stopped half a block down. The Eighty-Sixth Street trolley line went right through here. I had almost reached it when the car took off. Sister Agatha's screams got closer and closer. I could tell they were gaining on me, but I didn't want to turn around. I was just on the heels of the streetcar as it moved along the street. I grabbed onto a handle attached to the back side of the car, pulling my legs onto a small ledge. A couple of passengers seated inside at the very back saw me, eyeballing me curiously, but didn't alert the conductor. I looked behind to see Sister Agatha and Mr. Carson standing in the middle of the road, giving me a hard stare. I had done it! I'd escaped!

•••

It was only ten o'clock in the morning. With several hours to kill, I had to find something to do before coming home. After thirty minutes, I jumped off the streetcar and transferred to another line, making my way into the Lower East Side. I saw a pushcart vendor cleaning fish and weighing it for a woman at the corner of Orchard and Stanton Streets. I loved people watching in New York. An elderly street merchant slowly wheeled a pushcart jam-packed with crockery along the corner of Orchard and Delancy. I'm not sure what was livelier in New York, the curb-side merchants on the sidewalks or business inside the large department stores. On another street corner, a man was standing next to his cart selling peanuts. He had a very self-confident expression on his face as he hustled and bustled, trying to attract customers.

I continued along, walking by a food stand with an umbrella that read, "Red Hot Frankfurters and Ice-Cold Drinks." I glanced at the soda glass bottles in the box—Orange, Coca-Cola, and anything else you could think of. I walked by several people looking at various fabrics for sale at a table outside a store. Next, I passed the Bowery House, seeing a middle-aged man staring at the menu prices at the attached restaurant.

"What the hell! These prices are getting ridiculous," he griped. I stood next to him, and we both looked.

French Toast, Bacon and Eggs	*20 cents*
Hamburger Steak	*35 cents*
Lamb Chops and Beans	*40 cents*
Omelet	*25 cents*
Soup and Coffee	*10 cents*

The man turned to me. "Ten cents for soup and coffee. It used to be a nickel. The high cost of living is taking its toll."

I didn't say anything, just nodded my head.

"Oh, what am I talking to you for? What would you know? You're just a kid. Hey, shouldn't you be in school?" That was my cue to skedaddle. I scurried away.

I strolled into Lower Manhattan, heading along Mott and Mulberry Streets. There were street markets with pushcarts parked in front of the endless rows of small stores. The smells, the noise, and the whole sense of atmosphere were powerful. I wandered for another hour or so up Fifth Avenue, lost in my own thoughts. An older man listening to his radio sat on the terrace wall in front of the New York Public Library on the corner of Forty-Second Street. One pedestrian stood eating a hot ear of corn nearby a vendor with a corn cooking machine. A young girl with her pram was several feet away from me, watching her mother and other adults talking, rummaging, and buying items at a vendor stand. No doubt, in my mind, it was a very chaotic scene to observe at her age. She was probably only three or four.

A short while later, I was drifting through Times Square. When I got to the east side block of Broadway, between Forty-Fourth and Forty-Fifth, I noticed a massive sign. An extensive set of neon lights surrounded two gigantic nude figures, a man and a woman. The figures had to be several stories high. Between the figures, there was a waterfall that looked to be between twenty to thirty feet tall and over a hundred feet wide, with thousands of gallons of recirculated water. Beneath the waterfall was a huge long zipper sign that was probably several hundred feet, displaying scrolling messages. The Bond zipper was made up of what looked to be thousands of light bulbs, and just above the waterfall was a digital clock. Staring at this artwork, I felt like a deer in headlights.

The sign on the store read, "Bond Clothing." A second sign read, "Two Trouser Suits." Men's suits were displayed in the window. This was the most prominent men's clothing store chain in the country. As I ambled by, a salesman stood at the door trying to draw customers inside. "Men's suits! Get yer men's suits here! Starting at fifteen dollars!"

Another man walked up to the salesman. "Fifteen dollars, you said?"

"That's right, sir, and you get two pairs of pants per suit purchased."

"Okay, you've convinced me." The man stepped inside, with the salesman following behind.

I moseyed through a side street alley, glancing at a heavily faded poster on the side of a building that read, "Your wartime duty! Don't waste water. Do not use hose for washing your automobile. Do use water from a pail." It showed an image of a man on the left with a stern look using the hose on his car. On the right side was a man with a sparkling clean car and a beaming smile on his face.

I backtracked and changed my direction, heading south a few blocks. I walked by the Hotel McAlpin on Herald Square at Broadway and Thirty-Fourth. There was a small crowd of people standing outside the entrance. I did my best to step through everyone. Turning to look behind me for a brief second, I considered if I should take a different route. I ran right into a man coming out of the hotel entrance as I turned around. I looked up at him. He was black, probably in his mid to late twenties, and slightly tall at five-eleven. Several people were yelling at him, bearing cameras and waving items and pens nearby.

"I-I'm sorry, sir. I wasn't paying attention," I stammered.

I could still hear the crowd yelling. "We need to get a photo!" a voice shouted.

"No worries, kid. Whoa, what happened to your hands, son?" He stared at my knuckles that still had dried blood on them. I had totally forgotten.

"Uh. I had an accident at school."

"Can you look into the camera, Jackie?" another voice yelled.

"Well, maybe you should be home nursing those injuries. You take care, kid." Ignoring the crowd, he nodded at me and walked off.

"Mr. Robinson! Mr. Robinson! Can you sign this for me?" another voice yelled.

Several voices: "Jackie! Jackie!" "You gonna bring a championship to Brooklyn?"

The man turned back around. "Okay, guys. I only have a few minutes. I'll sign a few things and do some photos, but I have to get going."

As I walked away, I saw him posing for the news cameras and signing items for several people.

I headed south again and back through Lower Manhattan, making my way toward the Brooklyn Bridge. I found myself walking by City Hall. There were large groups of WWII veterans shouting and holding signs that read: "Is This the Dream Home Veterans Fought For? All We Want Is a Place to Live," "More Homes for Vets," "Veterans Preference for All City Housing," "Homes, Not Barracks," "East Midtown Committee National Citizens PAC," and "Fewer Titles for Moses. More Homes for Vets."

I went east in and around Tribeca, walking through the extensive Washington Market. This was one of the largest produce markets in all of Manhattan. It was mainly focused on Washington Street, but it trickled over into Fulton and Chambers Streets.

After heading back west, I had almost reached the Brooklyn Bridge when I decided to peek into the window of a hair salon. A woman sat in a chair getting a manicure while a giant contraption, which looked like the base of a light bulb, covered the top of her head. Very weird. After several more minutes of walking, I finally reached the bridge and entered the pedestrian walkway.

• • •

The walk across was just over two miles and took me an hour. I got off the bridge and arrived in my neighborhood of Brooklyn Heights. I went to a nearby pier and finally rinsed my hands in the East River. The blood was gone, but I was still sore. By now, it was after three o'clock and right about the usual time for me to arrive home. It took me about fifteen minutes to get to my neighborhood.

Approaching my block, I headed to my residence, a large three-story building with several apartments on each floor. I saw a car parked just in front I had never seen before. Probably someone visiting one of the neighbors. I ran up the stairwell to the second floor and stopped outside our apartment door. Just act normal, Johnny, *I instructed myself. I reached into my pocket, pulling out the key, and unlocked the door. I quietly closed it behind me, locking it back. It was quiet. Mom was probably sleeping. I tiptoed through the hallway to pass the kitchen but did not get very far.*

"Johnny!" my mother yelled.

I stared in horror to see Sister Agnes, Sister Agatha, and Father Jacob sitting at the kitchen table with my mother.

My mother jumped up and grabbed me by the ear. "You caused trouble at your new school! And you ran away! Where have you been?"

"Mom! I didn't do anything wrong! I—"

She slapped me hard against the face, knocking me onto the floor. I cried. The slap was bad enough, but in front of everyone just made it so much worse. I remained on the floor, my eyes once again filled with tears.

"I told you that you would be sorry, Johnny," Sister Agatha scorned me yet again.

Father Jacob stood up. He was very tall, middle-aged, and big-boned with a bit of a belly. He walked over to me and crouched down to my level.

"Johnny, I'm very disturbed at everything I've heard that happened today. You are squandering your opportunity at Saint Esther." He shook his finger at me. "If you don't straighten up, young man, we will have to expel you indefinitely."

"Oh, trust me," my mother said. "He will learn his lesson. I will discipline him accordingly. I'm so sorry about all the trouble he has caused, Father."

Sister Agnes and Sister Agatha stood up, and my mother walked them and Father Jacob to the door. They all nodded in agreement with each other before walking out. My mother closed the door shut.

"Get your ass in your room right now! Hurry before your father gets home."

As she shooed me into my room, I tripped. After stumbling up from the ground, I dashed into my room and locked the door. I buried my head into my pillow as I sobbed and sniveled. Not even ten minutes later, I heard the front door open.

"Where's that goddamn kid?" my father yelled.

"What's wrong, Sal?" my mother asked him.

"Don't lie to me, woman! I just ran into the principal and nuns out on the street! They told me Johnny caused a shitstorm today! Is he in his room?"

I heard his footsteps approaching.

"No, I already punished—"

I heard a loud shriek from my mother, followed by a crash.

"Don't you dare get in my way!"

"Get away from that door!" I heard my mother yell at him again.

"You bitch!"

"No! No! Get your goddamn hands off—" My mother shrieked in pain several times as I heard my father beating on her repeatedly.

My father was a man of few words, but many actions—violent actions. Born in 1895, he was thirteen years older than my mother, with a noticeable size difference. At six feet, my dad towered above my mother, who was just under five feet tall. He wasn't a big man, but he was lean and muscular. He had reached my door. I could hear him trying to turn the doorknob.

"Unlock this door, you little bastard! You hear me? We fought hard to get you in that school, you ungrateful shit!" I was paralyzed with fear and knew he could easily break the door down. I hadn't thought about the repercussions of my actions today. I assumed I was gonna get away scot-free. At that moment, I learned that everybody pays the price, no exceptions. He banged on the door several more times.

"Fine! Stay in there! I'm gonna have myself a drink. You better not come out for a long time, boy!"

I heard him walk away and into the kitchen. I knew I could wait it out. He would drink several glasses of scotch before eventually passing out and forgetting about what I had done. I had seen this happen many times in the past. I had witnessed him and my mother fight on several occasions. Billy once told me he had gotten a horrible beating from our father when he was around the same age as me now. Since then, Billy was always careful around him. I never once remembered seeing him go after Billy. He was the favorite, a model student who almost always did what he was told. Even when Billy argued with my mother, he knew how far he could push before knowing when to back down.

• • •

Two hours later, almost five thirty, I heard my mother knock on my door.

"Johnny, dinner is ready. I hope you've had time to think about what you've done. C'mon, time to eat."

Slowly, I opened the door and looked out into the hallway. I caught a glimpse of my mother's back as she returned to the kitchen. I could tell by her movement she had calmed down and it was safe to come out. The anger and beating period had passed, and we had moved on to the "let's talk about it" period. I came into the kitchen and saw my brother, Billy, sitting at the table.

"When did you get here?" I asked.

"Probably not long after you did. What happened?" He gave me a concerned look.

"He ran away from school," my mother said as she stirred a pot of pasta on the stove. "But don't worry about him, Billy. You focus on yourself."

Billy's eyes widened at me. I shrugged. No doubt he would talk about it with me later. My mother put two large bowls on the table a few minutes later, one with pasta and another with red sauce. In addition, there was a small plate of bread loaves. I saw the bruise on the side of my mother's face—small but noticeable. She looked stressed.

My father wandered in from the bedroom, a glass of scotch in his hand. "I'm starving. Alcohol makes me hungry. Ha!" He was definitely tipsy.

"I put extra butter on the bread since I know that's how you like it, Sal." My mother handed him the plate of bread. He took the plate without responding, pulling two pieces and setting them on the side of his plate.

"Tomorrow, cousin Jeanie is coming over for the day. I'll be gone early in the morning until the evening. I'm going to Jersey City with Louise and some of her friends. Billy and Johnny, you both will keep her company. Your father will be around if you need anything." She looked at my father. He nodded.

"Yup, I'll take care of her," he grumbled unenthusiastically.

Jeanie was thirteen years old, a year older than Billy. She was my aunt Louise's daughter. A couple times a month, my aunt would drop Jeanie off at our place while she and my mother spent time together around the city. She was older, so she didn't need much supervision. Billy and I would play board games or ride our bikes with her most of the time. When Jeanie first started coming over to the house several years ago, my father found her quite a bother. Over the past year, however, he seemed to get along quite well with her. He even told my mother she should spend more time with her sister.

"It's nice to get you out of the house, Mary. Ha! Then I can actually think without you being a nag," my father said in his drunken state.

My mother had a hurt look on her face, but she knew she had to take it from him. She got smacked around regularly, causing her to take it out on Billy or me, though mostly me. We all finished dinner with my father getting more drunk. He eventually went to bed and passed out after we cleaned the dishes. I started back toward the hallway to go to my room again.

"Hey, Ma, is it okay if Johnny and I take a walk around the block?" Billy asked her.

"I don't know. Johnny caused a lot of trouble today, Billy."

I stopped in the middle of the hallway, staying quiet. I didn't know how, but Billy always found a way to work magic. He was a smooth talker.

"I know, but it may help him to better think about his actions. I'll talk with him. I'll help him understand why he was wrong."

My mother quieted her tone to a whisper. "Billy, when you were young, you made trouble, but you've grown up since then. It's fine, but no more than an hour."

"Okay, Ma. Thanks." I heard him kiss my mother. A moment later, Billy came into the hallway and motioned for me to come out with him. He was definitely the favorite in the household.

• • •

I walked alongside Billy in the cool autumn weather. It felt good to be out of that apartment. I felt trapped. My parents had always had issues, but the added burden of being in Catholic school was just too much for me right now.

"What's up, Johnny? Tell me about what's goin' on."

I knew I could confide in Billy. My only wish was that we were closer in age, so I could hang out with him at school. He was the cool older brother—kindhearted, athletic, strong, talented, and nothing like me. Even though he was only twelve, he had gotten quite tall for his age. Less than two years ago, he was barely five-two, and now he was five-seven. I had only reached four-eleven recently. I'd hoped I would catch up to him. He'd been playing street stickball for years and could run fast. On top of his athleticism, he had a strong passion for music. He had his jazz guitar with him strapped across his body. He took lessons for the last year after convincing my mother into it when he had done well in school. Even though he had not been happy about transferring to a new Catholic high school, he was still maintaining his good grades.

"There's this kid in my grade, Andrew Clausen. He always teases and bullies me. Almost everyone likes him, the nuns especially. He has rich parents who donate a lot of money to the school. He's the one who got me in trouble. He always throws things at me and calls me names, but the nuns never see him."

"Ah, there's another kid in my high school, a tenth grader with the last name Clausen. He is rather popular. He's on the basketball team. He's not necessarily

a bully, but he is a bit of a condescending prick. He brags about his family, too, always talking about their money. I'm certain he's the older brother of this other kid you know."

I relayed all the information about what happened, from the beginning to the end. Billy listened patiently while I told my story.

"You had the nuns running after you down the football field. Jesus! I bet that was a sight to see." He snickered.

"It wasn't worth taking the beatings for it." I frowned.

"You're going to have to be strong and adapt to your environment. Change is inevitable, Johnny. Nothing stays the same. You will be at St. Mary's junior–senior high in another four years, and new teachers will be there. You are going to have to make the best of your situation. Make new friends and work harder at school. Don't let that kid antagonize you. Don't let him get to your head. Ignore his stupid words and pieces of paper. Only fight as a last resort. If it comes down to a physical altercation, you will need to stand your ground. The rest of the stuff is petty and not worth damaging your reputation for."

"How are you so calm, Billy? You never lose your cool. You're obviously Ma's favorite, and probably Pa's too."

"I'm five years older than you. I just have more experience is all. Johnny, I don't think Pa has any favorites. As much as Ma can lose her temper, Pa scares the ever-living shit out of me. I told you he beat me really bad once, right?"

"You did tell me about that, but I've never seen him do anything to you except yell. I've been whooped by him twice already. I thought he was gonna break down my door earlier and do it again."

"Whatever you do, don't cross him. Stay out of his way. I have a bad feeling about him. Something is off somewhere inside of him. Not sure if it's the drinking or something else. Promise me you won't confront him ever, okay?" He gave me a severe look, putting his hand on my shoulder.

"Okay, I promise." I nodded.

"Wanna hear a song?" He didn't wait for me to answer before busting out a tune I didn't recognize. I wasn't very knowledgeable about music anyway. He was all smiles as his fingers plucked and pulled at the guitar strings. After a brief moment, he broke out into a ballad.

"Mother dear, I'm writing you from somewhere in France,
Hoping this finds you well.
Sergeant says I'm doing fine, a soldier and a half,
Here's a song that we'll all sing, it'll make you laugh!
We're gonna hang out the washing on the Siegfried Line,
Have you any dirty washing, mother dear?
We're gonna hang out the washing on the Siegfried Line,
'Cause the washing day is here.
Whether the weather may be wet or fine,
We'll just rub along without a care!
We're gonna hang out the washing on the Siegfried Line,
If the Siegfried Line's still there!
We're gonna hang out the washing on the Siegfried Line,
Have you any dirty washing, mother dear?
We're gonna hang out the washing on the Siegfried Line,
'Cause the washing day is here.
Whether the weather may be wet or fine . . ."

"That was great, Billy, but I don't know that song."

"It's called 'The Washing on the Siegfried Line,' performed by The Two Leslies, aka Leslie Sarony and Leslie Holmes. It came out a few years after I was born. I remember hearing it on the radio a lot during the war." I smiled as he put his arm around me. We continued laughing and joking about various things that weren't important but made me feel better. We walked around the block a few more times before making our way back home. My father was passed out in the bedroom, and my mother was knitting in front of the radio. I said goodnight to her. Billy and I went to our separate rooms, and I drifted off to sleep.

• • •

I woke up at seven the following day—Saturday. I could hear Billy talking to my mother in the kitchen; they were always early risers. I rose sluggishly out of bed, headed to the bathroom, and took a quick shower. I came into the kitchen to see Billy and my mother sitting at the table eating breakfast.

"Johnny, I made breakfast. Aunt Louise should be here any moment with Jeanie. There is a covered plate in the oven. That's for your father, so don't touch it."

I nodded. A moment later, the buzzer rang. My mother rushed over to the door.

"Hey, Sister."

My aunt stepped inside, and, a second later, Jeanie appeared.

"Hey, Aunt Mary!" she said, giving my mother a hug. They all stepped into the kitchen.

"Hey, kiddos," our aunt greeted both Billy and me.

"Hi, Aunt Louise." Billy got up and gave her a hug. She kissed him on his cheek.

"He's gotten so tall. Wow. You will be almost as big as your father soon."

"Hi, Aunt Louise," I said, not wanting to get up from the table, but I did anyway. I walked over to her slowly and hugged her.

"You look rough. What happened to you?" she asked.

"Not now, Louise. I'll tell you all about what he's been up to when we're in the car."

Jeanie waved at both Billy and me. "Hi, Billy. Hi, Johnny. How are you all doing?"

I nodded at her. Billy went in for a hug. Even in the early mornings, he had so much more energy than me.

"Where's Sal?" Aunt Louise asked. Jeanie seemed to wince at the sound of his name. I still couldn't figure out if they got along or not.

"He's still sleeping. He drank several glasses of scotch last night. Hopefully, he will get up before noon. Okay, let's go. Billy, Johnny, you spend time with Jeanie while your father sleeps. Jeanie, there is still some breakfast left for you. Just don't touch the plate in the oven. Have a great day, kids! We will be back later tonight."

She and Aunt Louise left the apartment. Now it was just the three of us kids in the kitchen.

"So, what's new, Jeanie?" I asked. Billy sat down in a chair across from me.

"I've got some new drawings. Wanna see?" Jeanie was an avid artist. Her illustrations were pretty detailed.

"Sure."

She opened her large brown leather handbag and pulled out a sketchpad. She sat down in the chair next to me, moving aside some dishes to make room before placing the pad flat on the table. She flipped a few pages and held up a pencil drawing of the New York City skyline.

"That's really good," I said.

She flipped through more pages and showed another illustration of several kids playing stickball in an unnamed street. One boy was in the act of striking the ball while the pitcher's arm was stretched out, silhouettes of players in the background. The boy hitting the ball looked familiar.

Pointing to the picture, I said, "Is that—?"

"It's your brother."

She turned the pad in Billy's direction.

"I'm flattered." Billy smiled.

She smiled. She flipped through a few more pages. As she continued page-turning, I caught a quick glimpse of a drawing of a nude man who resembled my father. I reached over quickly to stop her.

"Hey. Why is that there? Is that—"

She yanked the pad away and closed it shut.

"It's nothing. That one's private."

"That looked like our father," I said, puzzled.

"You drew Pa?" Billy asked.

"N-N-No. That's just a sketch I'm doing for my art class. I forgot it was in there," she said nervously. Billy shrugged and ate his breakfast. I was still bewildered but decided to drop it, continuing my breakfast.

"Speaking of Pa, he will probably be up in a couple of hours. We should probably get some playtime in before that. You know how he usually makes us do chores and errands on Saturdays. You guys wanna go outside for a bit before he gets up?" Billy looked at both Jeanie and me.

I nodded.

"Yes, let's ride bikes. Do you still have that spare one?" Jeanie asked.

"No, but we have a skateboard." Billy got up, opening the door to the small outdoor patio.

He grabbed the skateboard and held it up, showing it to her. We all quickly finished our breakfast. Billy and I grabbed our bicycles—Jeanie with the skateboard—and headed out the door. We carefully brought everything down the stairs and out onto the street. Billy had a man's bicycle with the straight bar. I had inherited the woman's one from my mother; it had the slanted crossbar. A few neighborhood boys laughed at me several times when I rode it. Needless to say, I didn't like to use it much. Hopefully, I could inherit Billy's when he stopped using it. Jeanie was pretty good on the skateboard. Not too fast, but she had no trouble maintaining her balance. I had fallen off that thing a few times with several cuts and bruises to show from it. We all headed down to Prospect Park.

Twenty minutes later, we reached the park. We set our bikes down and sat on a bench side by side.

"I'm glad we get to see you a little more now, Jeanie," Billy said.

"Yeah, I know Pa wasn't too thrilled about your visits several years ago. Do you two get along better?" I asked, deciding to try and pry more into the subject.

"Yeah, we get along fine." Jeanie shrugged. "Why wouldn't we?"

"Well, I remember that one time when he—"

"Hey! I have some cool cigarette cards and matchbox covers," she interrupted. She reached into her bag, pulling out an assortment of colorful covers and cards. My mother had stopped smoking before I was born. My father smoked a pack of day, but I had never thought to look at them for stuff like this.

"Oh, I remember some of these when Ma used to smoke. Pa's cigarettes are all Lucky Strike, but Ma used to rotate several brands. I used to collect these when I was younger," Billy said.

Jeanie handed me a small stack of them. "You can have some if you want." She smiled at me.

"Thanks."

I examined them curiously. One card had a drawing of a beautiful dark-haired woman in a red outfit. At the top, it read, "Player's Cigarettes," and at the bottom "Claudette Colbert" with "Paramount" written in the bottom left corner. Another card pictured a circus clown holding a hula hoop with his feet broken through the cloth-covered hole of the hoop, the top reading "Taddy's Clown." I gazed at the side of another one of the matchbox covers, which showed a young man and woman holding hands on a roller-skating rink. I flipped to the other side, which read, "America's Most Popular Sport" at the top with a big "America Wheels" logo beneath. As I sorted through several more cards, I found a card with Charlie Chaplin on the front with the words "Player's Cigarettes" on top. The back showed the words "John Player & Sons," along with a small biography of the actor. I set it aside and continued to search through them. I found another card with a black man in a Brooklyn Dodgers uniform, who I immediately recognized. It was a black-and-white photo of him sitting on a bench, a large pack of Old Gold cigarettes blown up on a large table on the lower right part of the card. I turned it over to read the bio.

"Jackie Robinson, first baseman of the Brooklyn Dodgers, was born in Cairo, Georgia . . ."

I looked up at Billy and Jeanie excitedly and said, "I met this man! I met him yesterday."

They both gave me a look and giggled.

"Sure ya did, Johnny." Billy grinned.

"Yeah, of course you did," Jeanie teased me.

"No, when I walked around the city, I bumped into him. I'm being serious."

"Are you sure it was actually him? It could have been someone who looked like him," Jeanie said.

"No, I saw photographers and people asking for autographs. It was definitely him."

They both gave a surprised look that said they neither believed nor disbelieved what I had said.

"Can I have this one and the Chaplin?" I asked Jeanie.

"Sure!"

I smiled and put them both in my pocket.

"It's almost ten o'clock. We better get back home. Pa is probably up by now. He's gonna have some errands for us to run," Billy said.

"Yeah, he will probably have me help him do some cleaning inside too," Jeanie said.

I found it strange that my father would have Jeanie do cleaning chores. Mother did most of the cleaning around the apartment. I guess he just liked to put all three of us to work. It was only an hour or two, so I never complained much.

• • •

The three of us arrived back home at half-past ten. We carried our bikes and skateboard up, entering the apartment to see my father in the kitchen.

"Where you three been to? I got errands for you boys to do. Hi, Jeanie, how are you?" Sal said.

"I'm fine, Uncle Sal. How are you?"

"Good. I've got some things I need you to help me with in the house while the boys run some errands. Boys, here's a grocery list and some stuff I need from the hardware store. Make sure you get everything. Don't rush. I'd rather you make sure all the items are checked off first. Here's some cash and a little extra to get some sodas for yourselves." He handed me the two lists and gave Billy a stack of cash.

I put the bikes and skateboard away. It would be easier to walk and carry the items back. I'd once used the bike to bring back a carton of eggs and had dropped everything when I fell off, cracked eggs all over the street.

Father faced out to the patio and lit up a cigarette. "See you boys later. Get goin' now."

Billy and I scrammed out of there.

"See you later, Jeanie," Billy said, waving to her.

The two of us left the apartment. Billy talked to me about different songs that he was listening to. As usual, I had never heard of any of them. We had walked and talked for almost fifteen minutes when I reached into my pocket.

"Oh no," I said as I dug deeper into my pants.

"What?"

I pulled out the one piece of paper I had—the grocery list.

"I guess the other list for the hardware must have fallen out of my pocket. Let's walk back and look for it. If we can't find it, then we will just ask Pa to write it down for us again."

Billy shrugged. "Okay, that's fine. Pa said he wasn't in a hurry, so it shouldn't be a big deal."

We turned around. After several minutes of silence, I felt Billy nudge me with his elbow. I looked over to see him smiling.

"What?" I asked as he gave me a silly look. I put my hands up in confusion. He said nothing for a long moment, and then, suddenly, he broke into song. I shook my head, laughing. Not again, *I thought.*

"Today's the day that all us cats
Must surely do our bit
We all must do our share
So Uncle Sam can hit
Save up all your pots and pans
Save up every little thing you can
Don't give it away
Get some cash for your trash, yeah
Save up all that old newspaper
Save up high just like a high skyscraper
Don't give it away
Get some cash for your trash
In between we'll do some lovin'
Wide handsome turtle dovin'
Will you listen to me, honey
Get plenty of the foldin' money
Save up all your iron and tin
But when you go to turn it in
Don't give it away
Get some cash for your trash."

When he was done, he once again gave me that look. I stared in confusion.

"Do you know that one?" he asked.

"Nope." Shaking my head as usual.

"That one is 'Cash for Your Trash' by Fats Waller," he stated proudly. "You should listen to more music, Johnny."

I nodded at him. We had finally reached our apartment building. We went inside and ran back up the stairs. Billy stayed near the end of the hall by the staircase.

"I'll wait for you here. If you don't find the list, just ask Pa to write it down again."

I nodded, walked down the hallway, and unlocked the door to our apartment. I went inside, and there was no sign of Jeanie or my father. I wondered if they had gone out. I went into the kitchen and saw the tiny piece of paper that

I must have dropped on the floor. I picked it up, reading the hardware list, and stuffed it inside my pocket. I heard a slightly muffled groan. My ears perked up, and I stood perfectly still. A moment later, I heard it again. It sounded like Father. I tiptoed slowly and quietly down the hallway leading to my parents' room, which was at the end past Billy's and mine. I could see the door was cracked slightly open. As I got closer, I heard heavy breathing. I peeked through the cracked door. I could only see one side of the bed. I pushed lightly on the door, inching it open. My head was just inside, and I couldn't believe what I saw.

My father was completely naked and doing what looked like push-ups over Jeanie, who wasn't wearing anything either. I was confused and in shock, unable to move. I stared in fear. Jeanie's eyes were closed. Suddenly they opened and stared right at me. A look of horror covered her face. She gasped, "Oh! Johnny!"

My father turned to see me staring. "Goddammit, Johnny!" he yelled.

I ran into the hallway and back into the kitchen, unsure what to do. My body froze in fear. Within thirty seconds, my father had gotten dressed, marched from the hallway right up to me, and grabbed me with both hands, shaking me furiously.

"What the hell are you doing back here?"

I had never been more afraid in my life. "What were you doing to Jeanie!" I screamed loudly.

"You shut up, you little shit!"

I was terrified, and my only instinct was to scream.

"Stop that!" He threw me hard onto the floor. I landed on my back, the wind getting knocked out of me. He had both hands around my neck, and he was choking me. I tried to pry his hands off me, but I wasn't strong enough.

A second later, I heard Jeanie scream, "No! Let go of him!" She ran at my father from behind. He pushed her away like a rag doll, and she fell against the wall, landing on the ground. I felt the life going out of me as if I was about to pass out. Just when I thought I was about to lose consciousness, I heard footsteps.

Suddenly, I saw a hand swing a ceramic vase down onto my father. It shattered as it made an impact on the top of his head.

"You get your goddamn hands off him!" Billy shouted.

"Fuck!" my father screamed as he fell off me.

I looked up to see my brother standing over me. He grabbed my hand and pulled me up.

"I thought you of all people knew your place by now! I beat your ass several years ago. Don't you remember?" My father glared at Billy from the floor.

"Yeah, I do! I've been too scared to say anything since, but not today. You could've killed him! You're a no-good piece of shit!"

I had never seen my brother so upset in my life. Jeanie ran toward the door, screaming. My father lunged for her, but Billy stepped in his way to block him. He punched my brother in the face, knocking him backward. My father threw another punch, but this time Billy dodged it and connected with his own hit right to my father's stomach. My father—pissed off now—grabbed Billy with both hands and threw him across the other side of the room. Billy was strong, but he couldn't hold off much longer against my father. I was about to run outside after Jeanie for help.

The door flew open. A man, who I had never seen before, walked in. He wasn't a huge man—maybe five-ten or five-eleven and a hundred and eighty pounds. There was a strangely familiar sense about him. He looked like he could have been in his thirties.

"Get your hands off him!" he yelled.

My father turned. "Who the fuck are you? Get outta my place!"

The stranger grabbed my father and pushed him off my brother. Billy scrambled out of the way over to me. We both stared in astonishment.

"You're a piece of shit," the man said to my father.

My father lunged for him, and the two men struggled for control. My father was the bigger man, but the other man was younger and quicker and ended up overpowering my father onto the ground. He straddled his body.

"You are old and weak. I can smell your fear," the man said in a raging raspy voice. He started pounding at my father's face with lefts and rights. At first, my father blocked his strikes, but the familiar stranger eventually won. Without standing up, the man grabbed a heavy ceramic cereal bowl from the top of the counter.

"I've waited a long time for this day," he said before beating my father's head with that bowl several times. I grabbed my brother, Billy—both of us afraid—and we watched.

"Wh-who are you?" my father whimpered.

"Someone who knows a lot about you. Your actions have affected many people in my life. You're never gonna forget this day. I oughta kill you right here on the spot."

He beat my father bloody senseless. Several minutes later, he stood up. Billy and I looked at the man in horror.

"Billy, Johnny, don't worry. I'm not here to cause you harm. I would never hurt you. Never," he said.

"Do we know you?" Billy asked.

"Yeah, you kinda do. You'll learn one day." He put a hand on my shoulder. "Continue to be a good person, Johnny, and you, too, Billy," he said before exiting.

Billy and I stared at our unconscious father.

"What do we do, Billy?"

Billy remained silent for a long moment, deep in thought.

Finally, he responded, "We need to ring Aunt Loui—"

At that instant, Jeanie came running inside, followed by two police officers, both late twenties to early thirties of average height and build. They saw my father on the ground unconscious, a look of concern spread across both their faces.

"Okay, everyone, I'm Officer Smith, and this here is Officer Kent. What happened here?" he asked.

• • •

Almost an hour had passed, and both my mother and Aunt Louise had finally arrived home. When Jeanie had run off screaming, she had alerted all the neighbors about my father beating Billy and me. The police had been called, and Officers Smith and Kent came in.

I informed both of them about what I had seen my father doing with Jeanie. However, she didn't mention anything about my father and her in bed together, and actually denied it. Billy had not seen what I had witnessed in the bedroom, so he was unable to corroborate what exactly had happened there. He could only claim my father had attacked both of us.

Billy and I continued to explain in detail our stories to the officers. My brother and I had each seen the strange man who'd walloped my father. After several minutes, my father had become conscious again. He sat on the floor with his back against the wall, holding a bag of ice to his head and looking in very rough shape. The police called an ambulance to take him to the hospital.

The officers asked my father about the accusations. He said the part about him and Jeanie was not true, but he confirmed the unknown man who had beat him. Neither Jeanie nor anyone else in the building had seen the stranger—just me, Billy, and my father. He had disappeared without a trace. I still felt a strong connection to him. The police had the building and perimeter searched for him without success. When asked about what he had done to Billy and me, my father simply said it was a minor disagreement and not a big deal. Neither officer believed him. They could see how distraught Billy, Jeanie, and I were.

Aunt Louise and my mother were utterly dumbfounded at all the conflicting stories, not knowing who or what to believe. The medical team arrived and put my father onto a stretcher. A third officer came with them, and he handcuffed one wrist to that stretcher and rode with them to the hospital. My mother and aunt argued over my father, something to the effect that Jeanie wouldn't ever be allowed near him again. Aunt Louise was screaming furiously at my mother. She and Jeanie eventually left. After they had gone, I overheard the two policemen whispering to each other just outside our apartment in the hallway.

"Jim, I really don't know what to make of it," Officer Kent said.

"Jake, I agree. The youngest kid says he saw his dad engaging in sexual activity with the niece, but he's the only one who said it happened. Both the niece and father deny it. We can't pursue investigating that without the girl's mother's permission."

Officer Smith replied, "What about the mysterious fella that whooped the father? Do you think the boys and the man were lying about that? The man and the boys claimed they had never seen him before."

"Well, it's hard to say. Even if the boys had ganged up on their father, I highly doubt that either of them could have caused that beating. It simply isn't possible, given how large Mr. Sandes is. The girl didn't witness the man either; she was too busy getting help from the neighbors. Nobody else saw this guy."

Officer Smith scratched his head, continuing to ponder the situation.

"How could a guy disappear like that without a trace?"

"Beats me." Officer Smith shrugged.

The officers came back into the apartment minutes later to tell us that my father would be charged with domestic violence. He would also spend a night in jail after being released from the hospital. They took down statements from everyone and informed us they would contact us if they had any further questions. After they left, I expected my mother to throw a fit, but she was strangely quiet, barely saying a word. She looked like she was in shock.

Billy approached her and asked, "Ma, are you all right?"

"I need a minute, okay? Can you both maybe go inside your rooms? I just need to think is all. If you want to go outside, that's fine. Please, I just need a moment," she said. She had a very distraught look on her face. I had never seen her like this.

Billy nodded and motioned for me to go outside with him. We didn't go far. We sat on the sidewalk at the end of the block.

"I don't understand, Billy. I saw Pa with Jeanie. They were both naked. I don't—"

"Johnny, I can't deny what you saw, but you were the only one who saw it. Jeanie doesn't want to out Pa for whatever reason. She's probably afraid of him. I wonder how many times he's done it to her. I also wonder if he's done it to anyone else. Has he ever touched you, Johnny?"

I shook my head. "What about you?"

"Never," Billy replied.

"What about that man who beat him up? Do you think everyone else believes us that he was there?"

"I'm not sure. Only me, you, and Pa saw him. I honestly don't think even the police know who's telling the truth. The whole situation is confusing." Billy looked at me. "I didn't feel afraid of that man. I felt like I knew him. Is that weird?"

"No, I felt it too. It was some strange connection like we were bonded somehow," Billy said, staring up into the sky and pondering.

"Do you think we will see him again? Will he protect us?"

"Well, I wouldn't rely on him to protect us every time we get into a bad situation, but I do think that one of us will probably see him again at some

point. I just feel it." Billy put his hand on my shoulder and asked, "Are you okay, Johnny?"

I nodded, grabbing Billy. He wrapped his arms around me, and I buried my face into his shoulder and cried. He was more of a father to me even though he was barely five years my senior.

"I'll always do my best to protect you, Johnny."

In an instant, everything became blurry. The black pool reappeared turning into white, bringing things back into focus.

CHAPTER 36

I awoke, unsure of where I was for a moment. Despite the horrors of my past, my dreams had been so vivid. I could remember so many details. Now, being back in the present, I felt everything was crude, simplistic, and lacking flavor. It's as if I had been a young Dorothy in the colorful Land of Oz only to suddenly return back home as a lonely aged widower in a black-and-white world. I briefly forgot about the pain and torture I had been through with James's men. When your body takes enough of a beating, eventually it shuts down. You stop moving. You stop hearing. Your teeth clatter. You just focus on holding onto that little part of you that's left and not worry about the rest. The rest will be taken away at some point anyhow.

I had no idea what time it was or how long I had been lying on the cold hard floor. My whole body ached. I remained still for several moments, trying to regain my senses. I slowly raised myself up, looking around the room. There was nobody else around. The area looked like some kind of cellar, with crates and boxes everywhere. I also saw sandbags and a ton of crap.

Now I remembered—I was in the basement of the Kundali. I lethargically walked over to the door and turned the knob, but it was locked from outside. I looked for any type of object I could use as a weapon. As I thought my luck had run out, I came across a piece of loose brick in the far corner. The windows were high up, and I noted several stacks of boxes near the door entrance. I quickly moved one of the sturdy boxes just under the window, stood on it, and broke the glass with the brick. I quickly ran back to the other side of the room and hid behind the stacks of boxes, waiting, the brick still in my hand.

A couple of minutes later, I heard footsteps coming down the stairs. Then the door was violently opened, and two men stepped inside the room.

"Shit! He must have gotten out!" one of them said.

"Look over there. The window!" The second one pointed to the far end of the room.

One of the men rushed over to the window and looked out. The second man stood just in front of me. I brought the brick down onto his head and grabbed his gun from him before he hit the ground with a thud.

As the first man turned from the window to face me, I shot him right through his skull, a quick death. I didn't even wait until he had fallen before running back to the door and kicking over some boxes and crates to block the doorway. I went back to the window, stepping over the dead man's body and onto the box. I hoisted myself through the window, cutting and scraping my arms and legs on the broken glass. I rolled outside onto the dirt in the back lot of the Kundali. I could hear banging on the door from the inside. I only had a moment's head start. I staggered around the side of the building. The gun in my hand was only a six-shooter, so I had five bullets left at best. If anyone saw me from the front, I'd do my best to take as many out as I could before I dropped dead.

I was almost entirely out of stamina. Tripping over my own two feet, I dropped the gun. I glanced around, looking for it, but it was too dark to see where it went—no time to waste. I had to get out of here as fast as I could. I had gotten off the property and was running down the dirt road. I continued swaying left and right as I ran. Suddenly, I saw a car in front of me start its engine. Its lights were off, but a shadowy figure emerged from the driver's side. I reached for the gun, forgetting that I had dropped it.

"John, it's me, Calvin."

"C-C-Calvin. Holy shit. What are you—" I stumbled, falling onto the ground. He ran over to me, helping me up and into the back seat. He laid me down.

"Keep your head down," he said as he got in the car and turned around, speeding off.

I was delirious. "We can't go back to the restaurant. We can't—" I was having a hard time keeping my eyes open. "James will look—"

"I know, John. I know. I know a place where you can hide."

CHAPTER 37

JAMES

James heard a shot from his bedroom on the second floor. He sat upright, his mind immediately focusing on John. Lana was sleeping in the bed with him, though she had moved to the opposite side. They hadn't had any intimate moments in a while, at least not since John had arrived.

James quickly got dressed. Lana raised her head and asked, "What's going on?"

"You stay here," James commanded.

Lana wanted desperately to help John escape. She knew what they had been doing to him in the basement, but James had too many people watching her, and it wasn't safe for her to help him. She would not have been able to get down there unnoticed but assumed he had escaped. While looking out her window that faced the front, she spotted a small figure running away from the Kundali, and smiled.

When James got down all three flights of stairs, he saw several of his men in the room where John had been left to rot. He was furious when he did not see his prisoner's body anywhere in sight.

"He must have crawled out the window, boss," one of his men said.

"Fuck! Search the streets! Whatever it takes! Find him! Search this whole piece of shit town!"

He and his men ascended the stairs to the lobby and went out the front door.

"Look over there!" He pointed across the street. "Over there!" He pointed in another direction. "And over there!" He continued pointing in all directions.

"Rip up every goddamned inch of this area! Find him!" He walked over to the dead kid's rotting carcass that hadn't moved for days and kicked it. "Search under this goddamn thing if you have to!"

Several men went scouring the nearby neighborhood. A few more got into their vehicles, driving slowly to search nearby along the road.

"Let's get to the other side of town. He may wander back to the restaurant. If he does, we will wait for him there," James said as he, Randy, and one other guy hopped into a car and sped off.

James had gotten half a mile down the street. "He's on foot. He couldn't have gotten far. There's no way he'll escape us!"

CHAPTER 38

Minutes turned into hours, hours into days, and days into weeks. Nobody had found me. I barely moved the first few days, only getting up to take a sip of water or bite of food. I could stand just long enough to take a piss in a bucket in the corner if needed, but that was about all the movement I made. Eventually, I wandered a little within the building, not setting one foot outside. At first, I had stayed on the ground floor, but it felt safer to be at the top level as I slowly regained strength. I gazed out at the Indian Ocean from the top of the Dondra Head Lighthouse—seven stories up. This was a great vantage point. My view extended for miles, and I could spot anyone coming up on me.

I was still in rough shape. My bruises and cuts had healed a little, but I was achy and sore. I felt like one of my ribs had been broken, but it had gotten a little better. I think it was just severely bruised. I could breathe and walk, so I was content. Calvin had thought this would be a good place for me to hide out since hardly anyone ever came here. Occasionally, I would see headlights in the distance, but nobody came too close.

Calvin would come out every four or five days to deliver food and other necessities like medical supplies. No one else knew I was here, or so I thought.

CHAPTER 39

CALVIN

It had been almost a month since Calvin had transported John to the Dondra Head Lighthouse. It was the closest place that he could think of that was isolated. It had once been quite a tourist destination. Over the years, however, the increase in crime prompted visitors to stay away from this part of the island. Calvin knew he had to be careful making a weekly food and supply delivery run to John. James and some of his men had set up down the street, keeping an eye out. He had made sure to be diligent. He would meet the food supplier just outside town—about twenty minutes out—drive to John first before bringing the goods back to the restaurant. It was common knowledge that the food delivery trucks stopped feeling comfortable getting too close to this part of town. Generally, Calvin would rotate with the other workers to pick up the goods, but he had been doing it each and every time since John had been holed up in the lighthouse. Generally he would borrow one of his coworkers' vehicles to make the deliveries.

It was around nine o'clock in the morning, and Calvin, who was just about to leave the restaurant, was finishing some daily chores when James and five of his men walked inside.

"Okay, I'm tired of being patient. Where is he? I know you know where he is or where he went, at least."

"Who?" Calvin asked.

"Look what we found in his car, boss. Bandages and medical supplies," Bill said, holding up some of the items.

Calvin now felt stupid for not locking the vehicle doors.

James grabbed Calvin by the collar. Two other restaurant workers, who were inside, ran out when they saw what was about to happen. James didn't try to stop them.

"John. That's who! You got medical supplies. Don't lie to me, you little shit! I know he confided in you."

"I-I-I don't . . . I don't know where he is. M-M-Maybe he left to go home," Calvin said timidly.

James released him, laughing hysterically. He looked over at his men.

"Shit, that's funny. Isn't that funny? He went home." An evil grin plastered his face. He motioned for his men to grab Calvin. They slammed him onto the bar counter, glasses hitting the floor, shattering everywhere. James stood in front of him, staring into his face while he was held down.

"That man has had plenty of chances to run back home, and he never did! Why? I don't know. 'Cause he's too stupid? Too crazy? Maybe both? He didn't run away. No way in hell did that man run away. He won't run away from a fight, that much I'm certain of." He paused, giving an unhinged look. Calvin had never seen him so maddened before. John had opened up a fury inside this man no one had seen in a long time.

"You know, I expected John would come back to confront us by now. That's what I was hoping for, but I'm tired of being patient. It's time to end it once and for all. We're gonna have some fun with you." James stared at Calvin and gave him an evil smirk.

CHAPTER 40

I knew by the sound of the vehicle that it wasn't Calvin. I stared out into the distant road, catching a glimpse. Every now and again, people have a way of surprising you. One time out of a hundred, they turn out better than you think. I made my way down the seven flights of stairs slowly but surely. The car had started to park by the time I emerged from the main door. I held a sharp piece of a broken bottle in one hand.

"Just your favorite friendly neighborhood deputy inspector here." Inspector Khan said while staring at me.

"Where's Calvin?" I asked

"Calvin got caught doing his run for you. The food, the bandages. It just gave him away. James and his men took him."

"Where did they take him?"

"He's at that hotel where James and his men stay, probably in the same exact spot where they roughed you up. James figured you'd be back to confront him by now. He got tired of waiting. He knows Calvin is your buddy. Everyone knows. It's not exactly a secret."

I stared down at the bottle in my hand. "I'm gonna go to him."

Khan shook his head. "You think you're going to fight anybody with that damn thing?"

"I can get a firearm with it." I didn't give a shit how. I'd do whatever it took.

Khan reached into his vehicle, pulling out my holster and two guns along with the box of bullets.

"That's the only help you're gonna get from me, my friend," he said, putting the items down in front of me.

Khan went back to his car, turned around to look at me, and said, "I heard Kanish is thinking about doing his own personal cleanup with the rest of this town. You will want to be well on your way when that happens. If you're still standing, that is. But you didn't hear that from me."

He started to turn around before I called out to him again. "Khan, just one more thing. If you could do it for me, I'd appreciate it and promise to be out of your hair for good."

He stopped and gazed at me. I slowly walked over to him and whispered into his ear.

He shook his head. "I'll be waiting on your move," he answered before getting into the car and speeding off.

I might now owe this guy a favor if the time ever came. I didn't like it, but it was what it was. I was the kind of man who made my own rules. I didn't want to do favors, and I certainly didn't like to ask for any. Even though the odds had been heavily stacked against me, I had almost equalized the ratios. Even though I try to abide by my rules, I could still make mistakes. I only knew one thing for sure: James and every piece of shit who worked for him were all going to be better off dead. But what the hell, everybody ends up dead.

CHAPTER 41

JAMES/KHAN

Two men were holding Calvin down in a chair in the hotel lobby. James did not want to be reminded of his embarrassing mishap at securing his prisoner. Therefore, he did not want to bring him downstairs to the same room from which John had escaped.

"I'll stick a knife and cut up this pretty little mouth of yours, boy," he threatened, patting the sheathed knife attached to his belt. He unsnapped it and pulled out the sizable shining blade, sticking it inside Calvin's mouth, and rolling it around. Calvin's tongue was cut and blood flowed from his mouth.

"Don't fuck with me," he continued. "I'm not screwing around. This isn't fun and games. If you don't speak now, then I'll make sure you never speak again."

By now, Calvin was desperately trying to speak, but all that could be heard were moans and grunts. He was scared for his life as he had never been before.

"Hey! Stop it. Goddammit!" Senior Deputy Inspector Khan barged into the room, yelling. "He's innocent. Leave him alone!"

The men threw a couple punches at Calvin and threw him down onto the floor. He slowly crawled a few feet away, knowing he couldn't get anywhere even if he tried.

"Since when do you give a shit, mister fake lawman? All of a sudden, you have a conscience?" James raised his hands up in repugnance. "We killed Singh and the rest of his guys. We're not afraid to do the same to you. Now get out of here. This matter goes above and beyond your job description."

"Look, I know where he is. I don't want any more innocent people to get hurt. You can go after John, but leave that poor guy over there alone." He pointed at Calvin.

"Where is he?" James stepped right up to Khan's face.

"He's been staying in Galle Beach. That's where he was before he arrived here. He's staying at the South Side Inn right next to the beach."

James shoved Khan out of the way and screamed at his subordinates through the door. "Bill, Randy, you stay here and watch this kid. The rest of you boys, c'mon! We're going to Galle Beach!" The remainder of his men—seven of them—followed. Khan hoped they'd let Calvin go, but it didn't pan out that way. Khan watched James and his men get in their cars. He knew it was time to get the hell out of here. John had told him his plan.

CHAPTER 42

I watched from a distance. I wanted all the men gone so I could rescue Lana and Calvin. Bill and Randy, however, had stayed behind. I could handle two guys. James and the remainder of his men got into their vehicles. I waited until they were out of sight. Then I walked right through the front, kicking the door open. Calvin was lying on the floor, pretty scratched up. I heard Bill and Randy come running. The moment they entered the room, they stared in shock at the sight of both my guns pointed at them.

"Is the girl upstairs?" I said with a wide grin on my face.

They each reached for their guns, and I let them both have it, unloading several rounds into each.

Their bodies danced as the metal hit their skin, eventually hitting the wooden floor with loud crashes. I walked over each of their bodies and examined them closely.

"They're dead, Jim," I mumbled as memories of *Star Trek* filled my head. I retrieved each of their firearms, giving one to Calvin as I helped him up.

"I didn't think you'd come for me."

"Of course I did. I wouldn't leave you, my friend."

I looked up the staircase. "Lana! Are you up there?"

I heard footsteps running down toward me.

"Oh my God. I wasn't sure what happened when I heard those shots!" She came down the stairs, putting her arm on me. She quickly moved to the other side of Calvin to help him outside.

As we got out of the hotel, we saw Khan standing out front. I went over to him. "Take these two and keep your distance," I told him.

"What? What are you going to do?" Lana asked.

"John, you can't take them all by yourself. I won't let you do it," Calvin muttered softly. He was still shaken up, but he'd be okay.

"I'm gonna stay behind. Trust me," I said.

Khan and Lana helped Calvin walk away, and they eventually entered a building down the street.

I entered the Kundali again, stepping around dead Bill and dead Randy. I combed the place, ensuring no one else was hiding around inside the joint. Khan had bought me some time, sending them out on a wild goose chase to Galle Beach just as I had asked. I removed some loose bullets from my pants pocket and reloaded my magazine clips. I had two more fully loaded clips on me. It wouldn't be long before James and his crew got tired of looking and headed back here.

CHAPTER 43

I heard the vehicles pull up outside roughly two hours later. I could hear James talking outside. I stood on the second floor just near the stairs, my guns aimed at the front door, when two guys walked in. I fired several shots in their direction. They both toppled over. There were six more guys left, including James, if I was not mistaken. I ran up to the third floor.

"Fuck! He's here!" James, still outside, screamed.

Three more guys ran in and fired shots toward the area where I had been standing on the second floor a moment ago. They hadn't seen me go up another flight. I stood off on the far end of the balcony and waited. As they reached the second floor, I fired two shots from each gun at them, killing one of the men. I quickly ran into the room at the far end, locking the door behind me. The windows in this room overlooked the back side of the hotel. I opened up the window, leaving it like that. That wasn't going to be my route. I chose this room because it led to the rooftop. Quickly ascending the steps inside the room, I opened and went out the ceiling door to the rooftop.

CHAPTER 44

KANISH

For the last two hours, Kanish had been watching the Kundali from an abandoned building down the street. He knew things were coming down to the wire. Singh's gang had been wholly wiped out, and all that remained were James and a handful of his men—and that damned American. He had watched him go inside, heard gunshots, and saw him emerge with the kid from the restaurant and the woman, handing them off to Khan. He was disappointed in Khan for helping them, but he would deal with him later.

Now was his chance to make sure James and his gang—and the American—were all handled. He could see the American was standing on the rooftop of the hotel. James and his men had gone inside after him. He walked out the door and across the street. Crows were eating the rotting flesh of a small dead body that had been there for days. Kanish covered up his mouth and nose as he walked past. As he got to the steps leading to the hotel's front door, he saw two of James's men standing with their backs to him, looking inside the hotel.

"James ran up the stairs after him. Should we stay—" one of the men started to speak.

Kanish shot them each in the head. There were loud bangs as their brains splattered all over the ground. He didn't see anyone else on the ground floor—anyone who was alive. Just inside the doorway, he stepped over two more dead bodies. On the second floor, another body lay at the top of the stairs. He could hear James and some of the men on the upper floors. He ascended the first set of stairs.

CHAPTER 45

I stared down off the rooftop into the front to see Kanish walking up to the main hotel entrance. I heard two gunshots shortly after, followed by two thuds. I guess he was cleaning up the town just like Khan said he would. Now, I'd have to keep a watch out for him too. I stood on the far end of the rooftop and looked down. It was a long way to jump. I positioned myself out of sight from the doorway leading onto the roof.

The door opened, and one of James's men appeared. I unloaded several shots into him, and he fell back through the doorway. I stepped over the edge of the roof, finding a ledge on the side of the building. I was just out of reach from one of the third-floor balconies. It could be my escape route. I decided I was gonna jump. Just as I heard another man coming up the steps to the rooftop, I leaped off the edge of the roof to the balcony.

CHAPTER 46

KANISH

Kanish got to the second floor. He heard the commotion on the floor above him. He caught a glimpse of James and two more men trying to break down a door at the end of the hall as he stopped just below the top of the third floor. They got through.

He heard James yell, "He must be on the roof! You go up first."

A moment later, several gunshots erupted from above and then a loud crash.

"Goddammit. You go back downstairs and make sure he doesn't try to climb down from the outside," James told one of his men.

Kanish quickly ran down the stairs to the second floor before anyone could see him. A moment later, he heard the man's footsteps above him. He fired multiple shots into his back as he came down the stairs. The body toppled down the stairs loudly. He came down to the ground floor and went outside, walking down the steps in front of the building, and stood waiting.

CHAPTER 47

JAMES

As James peeked his head out onto the roof, he heard gunshots inside the building below. He turned around, momentarily confused. Within seconds, he heard more gunshots from a separate area on the side of the roof and turned his attention back. He looked around for John, but the rooftop was empty. He scanned down each side and saw a small bloodstain on one of the balconies of a third-floor room directly below. The door had been shot and kicked in. James ran back down the stairs into the room, running down the hallway toward the room John had entered.

CHAPTER 48

It was a leap of faith, literally. I flew for a few seconds and crashed up against the wooden balcony rail, somehow managing to grab onto it. My body was dangling three stories high. I used my upper body strength to lift myself up, my body tumbling over the other side onto the hard floor surface. I turned the doorknob from the outside. Fuck! It was locked. I took several shots around the door handle and broke the door down.

I quickly ran through the room and out into the hallway. I wanted to beat James out of here. I was down the first flight of stairs on the second floor when I heard James come back out of the far end room on the third floor. He fired shots in my direction. I kept running down the next flight of stairs to the first floor and out through the front door. I leaped off the stairs, landing on the dirt. Kanish was there, his gun pointed at me.

"Stop right there," he said. I raised my arms up.

My guns were holstered and not fully loaded, but I had enough of what I needed. A moment later, James came out the front door with his gun in hand. Kanish took a few steps back and pointed his gun at James as he got down the steps.

"Put your gun down too," Kanish said.

"I thought we had an understanding, Kanish," James said, looking at him.

"You're through here. All of you are."

James turned to me and said, "You got all nine of my guys, John."

"Nine? Randy, Bill, two on the ground floor, one on the second floor, and one on the rooftop. That's six," I replied. I looked to Kanish. "It appears you've been in on the action, too, huh, Kanish?"

"Every one of you has been a giant pain in my ass." He stared back and forth between James and me, rotating his gun at each of us.

I managed to take a few small steps backward, again using my little trick to create more distance between them and me. Suddenly, a shot fired. We all looked around. James staggered. Kanish looked over at him. I pulled my guns before Kanish had time to react.

Calvin popped his head out from down the street with a gun in his hand, the same one I had given him. "That's for what you did to me, James. You piece of shit," he said, giving a little victory dance. James clutched his chest, falling over onto his stomach.

"Well, you gonna kill me, too, son?" Kanish looked over at him.

"Nah, I'm fine now. I did what I needed to. I'm gonna go away now and just watch." Calvin ran away, out of sight.

Kanish and I stared long and hard at each other. Who knew we would be the last ones in this standoff? He had a look of hate in his eyes, a face I knew well.

"You're a sorry excuse for a lawman—" I didn't have time to finish my sentence as I saw his arm twitching slightly before raising it.

I unloaded, emptying the clips from each of my guns into his body. His body floated backward in midair, doing a backward somersault on its own as it hit the ground, landing facedown. I walked over to him, kicking his body over onto his back, staring at his face—eyes wide open and blood dripping from the sides of his mouth.

I turned around to see Khan, Lana, and Calvin walking toward me from down the street. Calvin had his stupid grin on his face. Khan had a slight smile, which didn't look bad to me anymore, and Lana looked relieved. She came over to hug me, holding me for a long moment.

"I'm so glad I'm with you. I promise I will help you. Before, when we were talking in the kitchen, I desperately wanted to tell you about what I saw happen to you outside when you were fighting Sonny. Your whole persona changed. Even your voice was transformed. You were a completely different pers—" A shot was fired, and I felt Lana fall against my body. Blood spilled from her mouth.

"No!" I held her for a moment before laying her gently on the ground. I kneeled over her. She was desperately trying to speak and managed to put her hand on the side of my face. "I wish I had a father figure like you in my life, John." Her arm dropped, and her head rolled to the side. She was still—breathless.

I looked over to see James lying on his stomach. He was struggling to keep his gun pointed at me. His hand was shaking. He pulled the trigger again. Nothing but a dull click. His gun was empty. I walked over and kicked the gun out of his hand. I bent over him and punched him in the face, grabbing his shirt by the collar. He tried to speak but could only grunt as his head dropped and lay motionless. I felt for his pulse. Nothing. He was gone but not before taking a soul who had displayed some rare compassion in this town. I didn't get a chance to get to know Lana, but I could say with confidence that she wasn't all that bad. She knew she needed to get out, but it just wasn't in the cards.

• • •

I shoveled two large holes in the ground on the property of the Kundali. I buried Lana first. I pushed the dead boy's rotted body as gently as possible with the shovel into the second grave and covered up the hole. I had found some spare plywood nearby to make crosses for each and stood them into the ground. I wasn't a holy man—not anymore. I don't know if Lana or the boy had been religious either, but this was my upbringing. I felt they needed to be honored somehow. I left the body of William James where it lay, letting the crows gnaw on his flesh.

CHAPTER 49

The following day I got up—not too late, not too early—at around eight o'clock. Calvin had made me breakfast and coffee. When I finished eating, I stood up to leave.

"You're not leaving yet, are you?" Calvin asked, looking worried.

"Not yet. I need to go see a man about a horse, or should I say, a woman about a horse."

"Huh? You and your horses." Calvin laughed.

"A horse is a horse, of course, of course. And no one can talk to a horse, of course. That is, of course, unless the horse"—I stared at Calvin, waiting—"is the famous Mister Ed!" I chuckled. "I'll be back. I won't leave without saying goodbye. I promise." I exited, leaving Calvin shaking his head, dumbfounded about my jokes once again.

I walked down the street toward Maleesha's building. I was surprised to see both her and Saanvi sitting on the outside patio. Saanvi looked at me. Maleesha obviously couldn't see me, but she faced her head in my direction.

"I'm surprised to see you outside," I said.

"The evil has been cleansed from the town. I can feel the changed energy. There is a little bit of hope now."

"What will you do, Maleesha?" I looked at both her and Saanvi.

"Not exactly sure, but perhaps we will try to make some sort of a life here."

Saanvi spoke now. "We thought of leaving this place, but she is not in a condition to deal with relocating. We have this house. We will try to make do, somehow, I guess."

I slowly walked up the steps toward them, pulling out a large envelope.

"I know this doesn't fix things, and it certainly won't restore your life to what it was before, but it's the only thing left that I can do. Please take it; use it for something."

I handed her the envelope with a jam-packed stash of rupees. It was the equivalent of a thousand U.S. dollars.

"We will find a use for it. We may take over the restaurant. We heard your friend over there was leaving town, and the owner isn't coming back. We can buy land and make this place a tourist town again. Hire some workers. Fix up this house. Maybe rent out some of the other buildings, bring the people back here again, the good people," Saanvi said, Maleesha nodded with approval.

I nodded, starting to walk away.

"John, you take care of yourself. I hope you fix things with your family," Maleesha said.

"Thank you."

I walked away.

• • •

I returned to the restaurant where both Calvin and Deputy Inspector Khan were standing out front.

"Well, John. You heading out?" he asked.

"Yup. Time for me to be on my way."

"What about you, Calvin? You stickin' around here?" Khan asked, looking over at the young man.

"Nah, I'm sick of this place. I'm going to find somewhere else—maybe I'll go to Colombo and try to get a better job, see what big city life is like. Anywhere is better than here. I've been stuck here too long."

"What about you, Inspector?" I asked.

"Well, I've alerted my superiors that the gangs have been wiped out. We need to start a clean slate. This time we will make sure the town stays honest. No more gangs or criminals. Your actions have had an effect on me, John. I won't lie."

I shook his hand, walked over to Calvin, and patted him on the shoulder. Then I got into my car and drove off into the sunset.

CHAPTER 50

I had to get one more look from the top of the Dondra Head Lighthouse before leaving. I had been too fatigued and beaten up to appreciate it before. I parked the car in front, walked up the spiral stairs—all seven stories of them—and stared out at the Indian Ocean, taking deep breaths of fresh air. After several moments, I sauntered back down again.

Staring at my useless cell phone again, I reached the ground level. The shadows underneath the stairs had piqued my curiosity. I switched on my phone's flashlight, and with it, I could see a sizable vent-like opening on the ground, an opening large enough to accommodate a human. Getting down on my knees, I examined it closer. Steps led down a larger staircase. Once I had climbed down a few stairs, I was able to stand up again and proceeded carefully. It took me down to a whole underground level. When I reached the bottom, I came into a large room. I directed my light to a stone wall. A skeleton lay against the far wall. I could tell it had been there for many years.

As I walked over to it, I saw some ripped clothing on the ground. To one side was a book. Picking it up, I dusted it off. The writing was in English. It was a journal. I opened to the first page:

Seaman Robert Jones
Born: April 9th, 1887
Ship: SS Perseus

I flipped through to the last entry:

1st March 1917

Day 127
It s been a week since our ship sank I feel weak and disoriented I crawled into a hiding spot to avoid hostile locals I found this box of precious items washed up on the beach When I am found I will be handsomely rewarded I miss my wife Antoinette dearly and hope to see her soon

That was the last thing written in the journal. I picked up the box, which was roughly the size of a small briefcase and made of wood. I opened it up, not believing my eyes. Gold necklaces, rings, and even a crown for a king. In addition, an assortment of colorful gemstones; one looked like a large ruby. At least twenty-five items inside. I closed the box, taking it along with the journal. I got back into my car and headed to Colombo. My flight was leaving tomorrow.

• • •

It took me roughly three hours. I had hit some traffic just outside of Colombo. I pulled up outside the Colombo National Museum, parked, and entered. The museum was a large white building—European-style architecture. It was late afternoon, a good thing since they were still open.

"Hello, who's in charge here?" I said as I entered the doors.

A woman looked at me. "Excuse me, sir, the ticket booth is—"

"I'm not here for that. I've got some artifacts here that may be of importance." I held the box out and opened it. Her eyes grew wide, and she quickly headed to an office down the hallway. I followed her.

"Marcus, I believe someone has something to show you, sir."

A man sitting at a desk came into view. He was Sri Lankan, looked to be in his early forties, with glasses.

I got right to it, placing the box flat on his desk, opening it with the contents facing him, put the journal down next to it, smiled, stood back, and watched. "I'm curious about my discovery."

He picked up his phone, punched a few buttons, and spoke into the speaker. "Diane, I need you to look at some items for me, please. It's important."

"Okay, I'll be right there," the female voice said on the other line.

"Our head curator, Diane, is coming by to examine these. She will have a better idea about the details of the items," Marcus said.

A few minutes later, a woman who appeared to be early- to midthirties approached from down the hall. Marcus showed her the items. She gasped.

"Where did these come from?" she asked.

"I found them next to a human skeleton in an underground chamber at Dondra Head Lighthouse. If you look in that journal, you will see this guy was a sailor in the early twentieth century. The last entry is from the year 1917," I responded.

She picked up the journal and started flipping through the pages, scanning them intently. After a moment, she looked up and said, "Let's take these items to my office. Please follow me."

Marcus and I followed her down the hallway and into her large office. She had ample open space with a large table in the center, antiquities, and paintings all over the place. Diane placed the box and journal on a large table in the center of the room. She pulled out a sizable microscope from one of her shelves, took a ruby from the box, and placed it under the scope. She examined it for a moment.

"It's definitely real," she said as she took several more minutes examining some of the smaller gold pieces she could fit under the scope. "These are real, as well."

She walked over to her computer and punched at her keyboard quickly, reading the screen.

"The SS *Perseus*, the first of a class of nine vessels of the Perseus class, was built in Belfast between 1908 and 1913 for the Ocean Steam Ship Company.

The vessel was destroyed by a mine laid by the German SMS *Wolf* vessel approximately eleven miles west from Colombo, Ceylon, now Sri Lanka. The ship was on its way to Yokohama with cargo. So that explains where the man came from, but these items are much older than a hundred years.

"I think these items may be a part of Zheng He's treasure—he was a Chinese explorer. These items have been missing for over six hundred years. I don't know how this sailor got them, but I'm pretty sure that's where they came from. We need to have authorities examine the area where you found the body. There may be more items and clues."

"No one has been to that lighthouse in many years. What were you doing there?" Marcus interrupted, looking at me.

"I just needed a place to get away from people, I guess."

"That area has had a lot of criminal activity over the last several years, so it's remained relatively uninhabited. I guess no one has gone to examine the underground part since this man died." He had a look of astonishment on his face.

"We need to call and have this place excavated and searched before anyone else finds anything," Diane said.

"What is your name, sir?" Marcus asked.

"My name is John Sandes. I've been visiting the country for the past couple of months. It was just a bit of dumb luck on my part finding it." I didn't want to mention any gang activity I got mixed up in. "Look, I'm glad it's of value. I figured this was the best place for it, so that's why I brought it. I'm going home tomorrow, so I'll get going and leave you experts to it."

"Mr. Sandes, thank you so much for this generous donation. It will greatly help the museum and add value to our collection. I would like to wire you some funds to your bank account for your troubles. It's not much compared to the value of this treasure, but I insist." Marcus led me down to another office where the accounting department was. I gave them my wiring information, deciding that was the best route to take. When that was done, I stepped back out in the lobby.

"Do you mind if Diane and I get a photo with you, sir?" Marcus asked.

"Um, sure."

The three of us posed with me in the middle, and another staff member took a photo with a professional-looking camera; the flash nearly blinded me. They thanked me. I thanked them for the money, and I went on my way. I was going to find one last beach somewhere in Colombo where I could relax before I left tomorrow.

CHAPTER 51

I checked into a hotel in Colombo and immediately headed off to get some swim time at one of the nearby beaches. It felt good to get in the water again. Even if I still hated myself in shorts, it was worth it for the exercise. After I had gotten a couple hours in the water, I ran back to the hotel, hoping no one would spot my skinny bare legs.

I showered, dried myself, and put on a comfortable pair of long pants again. I headed downstairs to the hotel restaurant and consumed a huge dinner. It was six o'clock in the evening, and my flight was very early in the morning, a three forty-five departure, to be exact. Now, I was going to try to get some rest.

I didn't sleep very much. I napped until maybe one o'clock in the morning, got up, took a quick shower, and made some coffee. Taking a taxi, I arrived at Bandaranaike International Airport at one forty-five, precisely two hours before my flight departed. I was gonna be in transit for over twenty-four hours. My first flight would connect to Hamad National Airport in Doha, then it was off to Heathrow in London for an almost ten-hour flight to Seattle.

I arrived with just a light backpack and a carry-on duffle with no bags to check. I had ditched the firearms and bullets, giving them to Deputy Inspector

Khan. Hopefully, he would go down the right path and be an honest lawman. I got through airport security within thirty minutes; it was surprisingly crowded. Most of the airport shops were closed except for one restaurant. I walked over and sat down at a table not too far from my departure gate.

The server came over and asked what he could get me.

"Just a large black coffee, please, and a bottle of water."

A few minutes later, he was setting my drinks down. He stared at the television and pointed at it. "Isn't that you?"

I looked up to see the photo of me taken with Diane and Marcus from the museum.

The male news anchor's voice spoke: "John Sandes, an American tourist, discovered priceless items from Chinese explorer Zheng He's treasure expedition, which date back more than six hundred years. The items were discovered at the Dondra Head Lighthouse. The details are still being investigated as to how they arrived there. The lighthouse has been mostly abandoned for the last thirty years. Still, the items were discovered in an underground chamber next to the skeletal remains of an English sailor who died over ninety years ago. Authorities and archaeologists have searched the area extensively over the last several hours. They have found some more items, as well. It is believed there are many more valuable items buried off the coast where the ships sunk—"

"Jesus Christ!" I stared in shock. I continued watching.

Marcus appeared on the television. "We are very grateful for Mr. Sandes's discovery. He has helped unravel an ongoing mystery that has had many wondering for the last six hundred years. There are still lots of questions and investigations to be done, however."

"Wow! You're quite a detective there. How did you know where to look?" the waiter asked, breaking my concentration from the screen. My initial shock quickly transformed into horror at the thought of my newfound fame.

"It's a long story. I don't have time to go into it right now. Hey, can I get an appetizer? Some wings would be nice," I said, doing my best to shoo the server away. He nodded and ran off.

I wasn't in the mood to be famous. Having my face plastered all over the news didn't make me feel comfortable. At least I was getting out of the country, though. Things would be back to normal once I returned to the USA. *Wait a minute*, I thought to myself. I remembered there was free Internet at the airport. *Now let's see if it actually works*. I pulled out my phone and entered the web address of my bank. Success. I couldn't remember the last time I had accessed the Internet. I entered my username and password and waited several seconds, and I stared in surprise at my balance. An extra twenty thousand U.S. dollars had been deposited by the museum. That was no small sum. I was expecting maybe a few hundred dollars, but as Marcus said, this was very small compared to what the treasures were worth. And from the sounds of it, my discovery led them to find more of it.

Fifteen minutes later, the waiter returned with my wings and drinks. I nodded in approval. I hadn't had wings in ages. The aroma of the sauce made my mouth water. I took a big bite, my hand getting all saucy, and the spice made my forehead sweat. I finished the food, slurped down the coffee, and gulped down the water.

My mind wandered back to the dream I had when I was beaten up in the basement of the Kundali. My late father was a bastard. I knew it, my late brother knew it, and my late mother knew it. I still never learned the identity of that man who came in to save Billy and me. He was probably not even alive anymore, although if he was, he would be in his eighties by now. He alluded that I would find out who he was one day, but it never happened. I guess that's a mystery I'll never know. I stood up and walked to my gate, where I waited until I boarded.

EPILOGUE

John Sandes did not see the other television screen in the seating area next to his gate. He had just boarded a moment earlier. The CNN channel was on. A female anchor spoke: "An American tourist visiting Sri Lanka discovered several items of precious valuables from a six-hundred-year-old voyage lead by Zheng He, a Chinese mariner, explorer, diplomat, and fleet admiral during China's early Ming dynasty. He was originally born as Ma He into a Muslim family and later adopted Zheng's surname. He led expeditionary treasure voyages across Southeast Asia, India, Western Asia, and East Africa from 1405 to 1433. The items were found in a lighthouse, specifically the Dondra Head Lighthouse, which was constructed in 1887—"

The End

ABOUT THE AUTHOR

Joseph, a native of Manhattan, New York, moved to Asheville, North Carolina at the age of eight, where he spent the majority of his childhood. His life has since taken him across the United States, Canada, and Europe, shaping his global perspective and fueling his passion for storytelling. A dedicated traveler, Joseph finds inspiration in international affairs, film, pop culture, photography and the unique atmospheres of the cities he explores—often while walking their streets or relaxing in coffee shops.

Joseph holds an impressive academic portfolio, including a Master of Arts in International Relations, a Master of Arts in Linguistics, a Bachelor of Arts in Linguistics & Russian, and an Associate of Applied Science in Information Systems. His writing seamlessly blends intellectual depth with vivid storytelling.

In 2021, Joseph made his literary debut with Left For Death, captivating readers with his gripping narratives. His forthcoming book, Unleash the Fury, promises yet another thrilling journey for his audience.